Shack Island Summer

PENNY CHAMBERLAIN

PRESS

WINLAW, BRITISH COLUMBIA

LIBRARY AND ARCHIVES CANADA CATALOGUING IN PUBLICATION

Chamberlain, Penny, 1958–, author
　　Shack Island summer / Penny Chamberlain.

Issued in print and electronic formats.

ISBN 978-1-55039-175-6 (pbk.).—ISBN 978-1-55039-243-2 (pdf)

　　I. Title.

PS8555.H289S53 2015　jc813'.6　C2014-907210-4　C2014-907211-2

This book is a work of fiction. Names, characters, places, and incidents are either the product of the author's imagination or are used fictitiously.

Sono Nis Press most gratefully acknowledges support for our publishing program provided by the Government of Canada through the Canada Book Fund and the Canada Council for the Arts, and by the Province of British Columbia through the British Columbia Arts Council and the Book Publishing Tax Credit, Ministry of Provincial Revenue.

Edited by Barbara Pulling
Copy edited by Dawn Loewen
Proofread by Audrey McClellan
Cover and interior design by Frances Hunter
Cover photo by Cleary Donnelly

Published by
Sono Nis Press
Box 160
Winlaw, BC V0G 2J0
1-800-370-5228

books@sononis.com
www.sononis.com

Distributed in the U.S. by
Orca Book Publishers
Box 468
Custer, WA 98240-0468
1-800-210-5277

The Canada Council　Le Conseil des Arts
for the Arts　du Canada

Printed and bound in Canada by Houghton Boston Printing
Printed on acid-free paper that is forest friendly (100% post-consumer recycled paper) and has been processed chlorine free.

To my sister, Pam, and brothers, Greg and Jason

CHAPTER 1

Sent Away

The bus rumbled to a start, lurched into reverse, and backed slowly out of the loading bay. Through the bus window, Pepper could see her mom—hugely pregnant in a flowery summer dress—and her dad, with his horn-rimmed glasses, short-sleeved shirt, and pocket protector. They waved from the sidewalk. Pepper slouched down, pretending not to see. She was convinced her family was the most boring family in the entire world. Her adoptive family, that is.

She turned to look at Everett sitting beside her. His glasses constantly slipped down his nose so he was always pushing them up again. Everett was her brother. Well, her brother from her adoptive family. Not a real brother. Not a blood brother. There was no question of mistaking him for her real brother. None at all. His hair was dark and lanky. He was pale, like a weedy plant trying to grow without sunshine. He was shy. He was studious. And he rarely laughed.

Pepper, on the other hand, had fiery red, curly hair. She had freckles and an enthusiastic, pig-snorting kind of laugh. People called her whimsical. They said she had an overactive imagination. It didn't bother her at all.

Pepper knew exactly why Everett was coming with her. Her parents thought she was too young to make the trip on her own. Everett had been sent to keep an eye on her. He was fifteen, only three years older than she was, but he was more serious than most grown-ups she knew.

Everett poked her in the ribs with his elbow. "Wave to Mom and Dad. They're right outside the window."

Pepper gave a slight wave as the bus pulled out of the depot. Just as it turned the corner, she allowed herself one last glance back at them. They were still waving. Despite herself, she felt her eyes mist over a little and a lump form in her throat.

All along the city streets, Canadian flags hung from storefronts in honour of Dominion Day. It was July 1, 1969, a national holiday. People everywhere were in a festive mood. Everyone, it seemed to Pepper, except for her. She couldn't think of a time when she'd felt more miserable.

She was going to Shack Island, an island far away off the coast of British Columbia, an island she'd never been to before. It was, as her parents had told her, where her grandma went to paint every summer. Now she was being sent there too. It wasn't that she didn't like the idea of swimming and fishing and walking barefoot in the sand. That part sounded fine. She just didn't like being sent away.

Pepper stared out the window. Ever since her mother had announced she was pregnant, all anyone wanted to talk about was the baby. It was always, "After all these years, what a miracle! Won't it be nice to have a baby in the house again? I think it's a girl. I just have a feeling. What shall we call her?" It was as if Pepper had suddenly become invisible.

Her parents had thought after Everett was born that they couldn't have another baby. That's why they'd adopted her. They wouldn't give her any details about the adoption, even when Pepper asked them directly. The only thing they'd say was that out of all the little girls they could have picked, they'd picked her. As soon as they'd seen her, they told Pepper, they knew she was going to be their own special girl.

Pepper had believed them. She'd lived with them almost her entire life. Grown up in their house. Called them Mom and Dad. She couldn't remember anything from before the adoption. Life with her adoptive family was all she knew. And during that time Pepper had never doubted that they loved her ... until her mom became pregnant. Then, suddenly, it seemed like they weren't interested in her anymore. They didn't actually come out and say it, but Pepper knew all the same.

First they'd moved her things upstairs to the attic, and they'd turned her old room into a nursery. The attic had dusty trunks and boxes piled up on one side. The air smelled stale. The floor, the walls, the ceiling: everything was bare wood. There wasn't even a place to hang her clothes. She didn't want the room in the attic. She wanted her old room. But her parents were firm. They told her they needed to have the baby in the room next to them so they could look after it in the night.

Then they'd missed seeing her sing "Yellow Bird" with the school choir in the music festival. Pepper didn't have a solo like Marcy Meadows, the teacher's pet, but she'd worked hard to memorize "Yellow Bird," and she knew all the actions. She'd been practising for weeks. During the performance she searched for her mom and dad in the audience. They weren't there. Later her mom said she hadn't been feeling well and had gone to see the doctor. Pepper had stomped up to her room (in the attic) and thrown herself on her bed. She hadn't come down for dinner, even though it was spaghetti and meatballs.

And now this, the final straw. They were sending her away for the summer. Pepper had been hurt when they first brought it up. She didn't want to go away, she'd told them. Why couldn't she stay home? She could help her mother around the house, she'd pointed out. The doctor had said her mother should take it easy. She was tired every day. Her ankles were swollen. They needed Pepper. Couldn't they see that?

Apparently not.

"You go and have fun," they'd said. "Everett will go with you."

As if that made it any better.

Pepper watched the passing prairie landscape from the bus window. She caught a fleeting glimpse of her own reflection in the glass. It was almost transparent, floating like a ghost over the green fields. Her hair formed a hazy, crazy cloud around her face. Her freckles looked like measles. Pepper grimaced, and the reflection grimaced back at her, revealing a distinct gap between its two front teeth.

Beside her, Everett was reading a magazine.

"Whatcha reading?" she asked.

"*Popular Science.*"

"What's the article?"

"The experiments the astronauts are going to do on the moon."

"On the moon? How are they going to do that?"

"When they land on it, of course!" He looked at her sharply. "You do know about Apollo 11, don't you? Men going to the moon? Less than a month away?"

"Of course I do." How could she not? The moon mission was all Everett had talked about for months. She just hadn't paid too much attention to the details. "What kind of experiments?"

"There's one where they're going to use special quartz reflectors to bounce laser beams back to Earth to get accurate measurements of distances between the Earth and the moon, and between continents to measure continental drift ..."

Pepper stopped listening. She leaned her head back against the seat and rolled her eyes. There was no question about it. Her family was the most boring family in the entire world.

Take her mom. She was the kind of mom who tended a vegetable garden behind the house, canned fruit for the winter, and cut her own hair to save going to the hairdresser. She wore cat's-eye glasses and squinted a lot. She made her own clothes—and Pepper's too. Which was not a good thing. Pepper looked down at her plaid pedal-pushers. They were yellow and orange and green, cropped just below the knee. They looked like something an old lady would wear. The worst thing was that her mom had made a pair for herself as well, but with a stretchy bit to go over her pregnant stomach. Her mom liked it when they both wore their pedal-pushers on the same day. That was Pepper's mom's idea of fun.

Pepper's dad worked in an office downtown. He drove a station wagon. He called it "the wagon," which always

11

made Pepper cringe. Especially if he said it in front of her friends. After supper every night he would fall asleep in his La-Z-Boy recliner with the newspaper over his face.

Several of Pepper's friends had been to Disneyland in California. They'd seen palm trees and the sidewalk of stars on Hollywood Boulevard. They'd stayed in hotels with room service. Marcy Meadows, the teacher's pet, had even flown in a plane all the way to Paris, France. The only holiday Pepper's family ever took was driving "the wagon" from their home in Edmonton to the West Coast to see her grandma. Grandma was her father's mother, and the only grandparent she had (by adoption, of course). The trip never involved staying in hotels overnight. Oh, no. They slept in pup tents along the way and packed an old hibachi barbecue.

They always went for one week, and they stayed in Grandma's main house in Nanaimo, a mill town on Vancouver Island. Grandma grew dahlias along the fence in her front yard, and, like Pepper's mom, she kept a vegetable garden in the back. There was a piano in the living room and a Ping-Pong table in the basement.

But this time was different. This time she and Everett were going for the whole summer, and they were going to stay at Grandma's summer place, miles out of town. It was just the right size for three people, Grandma had said on the phone, and Shack Island was a wonderful place to spend the summer, a special treat.

"What are we going to do there?" Pepper had asked.

"Swim. Fish. Play on the beach. You'll have a great time. You'll see."

Pepper wasn't convinced. Being sent away for the summer wasn't her idea of a special treat.

Not only that, it would take ages to get there. First there was the long bus trip. They'd even have to sleep overnight on the bus. Then another bus out to the ferry, and then the ferry from Vancouver to Nanaimo, where Grandma would pick them up.

Pepper squirmed in her seat, trying to get comfortable. All she could see were miles and miles of flat prairie. The monotony of the landscape made her feel fidgety and impatient.

"Do you want to play a game?" she asked Everett.

"I'm reading."

"You must have read that article by now!"

"This is a new article. And after I've read everything in this magazine, I have a whole bunch of other ones I've brought with me."

Pepper groaned, but he ignored her. So she tried to amuse herself by making up stories about the other people on the bus. The young hippie couple with their tie-dyed shirts and long hair were moving to the West Coast to build a tree house so they could live right in the middle of the forest. The pretty young woman in the purple suit was running off to meet her boyfriend and get married. She probably had her wedding dress in her suitcase. The bus driver had two wives, in two different cities, and seventeen kids between them. It didn't take long for Pepper to make up stories about everyone.

Next she rummaged through her duffel bag and found the brown bag lunch her mom had packed.

"You're supposed to save that for later," Everett said.

"I'm hungry now. Besides, there's nothing else to do."

Everett shrugged and went back to his magazine.

Pepper ate the oatmeal cookies first and then the tomato

sandwich. She left the apple and the carton of milk for later.

Some brothers would at least talk to you, she thought, as she crumpled up the wax paper and stuffed it back in the bag. Some brothers would make an effort. She closed her eyes and imagined the perfect brother. The perfect brother would be tall and strong. He'd tell good stories, and he'd *want* to spend time with her. He'd be handsome. Popular. Outgoing. But most of all, he'd be exciting.

And the perfect mom and dad? Well, right off the bat, they'd be rich. And glamorous. They'd have a big house. Her mom would be pretty and well dressed, with thin ankles. The perfect dad would drive her to the Dairy Queen whenever she wanted, and it wouldn't be in a station wagon, either. It would be a fancy sports car. But most of all the perfect mom and dad would never send her away because of a stupid baby.

Pepper opened her eyes and stared at the seat in front of her without really seeing it. Maybe her real family, the family she'd been born into, *was* the perfect family. It was possible. More than possible, even. The longer Pepper thought about it, the more likely it seemed.

Pepper had wondered about her real family off and on since she was small. But lately she'd been thinking about them more and more. Now the thought made her even more restless. She stretched her legs out. Then she pulled them up and sat cross-legged for a while. She turned this way and that.

"Stop squirming. You're poking me," complained Everett.

Pepper huffed loudly and turned away, pushing herself up against the window as far away from him as she could get.

That's when she noticed the book. It was a small paperback wedged far down between her bus seat and the side of the bus. She pried it out with some difficulty and read the cover. *How to Make ESP Work for You*, by Harold Sherman. "ESP" was printed in large, swirly, black-and-red-patterned letters. Just looking at the psychedelic pattern made Pepper feel a little dizzy. In smaller letters underneath she read, "*All of us have within us an incredible mental power that can change our lives overnight. If you are ready to explore this miraculous 'New' dimension of your mind, read this book.*"

Tingles of excitement raced up and down Pepper's spine. Yes, she thought. She *did* want to tap into the mysterious powers of her mind. That was exactly what she wanted to do!

CHAPTER 2

The Incredible World of ESP

Pepper flipped the ESP book over and read the back cover. *"Have you ever had a premonition that something was going to happen—and it did? Have you suddenly thought of someone whom you have not had in mind for months or years, only to get a letter or a phone call from that person, or to run into him at an unexpected time and place? Have you had a strong urge to do or not to do something, and followed your urge, later finding out that subsequent events proved your urge was right? Have you had a vivid dream or vision of some event which later came to pass?"*

Pepper's pulse quickened as she read on. *"If any of these experiences have been yours, it is possible that you have had a manifestation of what is today called extrasensory perception. This book is positive proof that ESP works ... and it can work for you."*

When Pepper read that part, a shock ran through her. There were times when she *had* wondered if she had ESP.

One time, for instance, she'd known, absolutely known without a doubt, that the teacher would call on her first thing that morning to present her book report in front of the class. And that was exactly what happened! Another time, on a cold winter morning, she was rushing to go outside. She threw on her coat and pulled on her hat. But that morning, instead of blindly shoving her feet into her snow boots as usual, she did something she'd never done before. She stopped herself and grabbed a flashlight instead. Then, very carefully, she picked up one of the boots between one finger and her thumb, and looked inside. There, nestled right down in the toe of the boot, was a small grey mouse! Pepper squealed and dropped the boot. The mouse ran out. It scooted across the floor and disappeared into a crack in the baseboard. Ever since, Pepper had wondered what had made her check her boot that morning—the only time a mouse had ever been hiding inside. It had to be ESP. And if Pepper *did* have special ESP powers, maybe this book could help her develop them even more. Just imagine what she'd be able to do then!

What incredible good luck to find this book, Pepper thought. But what if it was more than luck? Maybe she'd been meant to find it. Something mysterious had made her pick this particular seat on the bus, when she could have just as easily picked another. She started flipping through the pages, skimming as she went.

Finally, on page sixty-six, she found what she was looking for: how to read people's minds. It was all laid out step by step. Pepper read and then reread the sequence, trying to commit it to memory.

Step one: Get in a comfortable position.

Step two: Lift one leg and then relax it. Lift the other leg and then relax.

Step three: Lift one arm and then relax it. Lift the other arm and then relax.

Step four: Release all the tension in your trunk, starting with the hips and going up to your head. It should feel like a wave of lightness going up your body.

Step five: You should no longer feel aware of your physical body. Imagine a blank, white movie screen in a dark room.

Step six: Now think of the person you want to send a message to or receive one from. Then wait for images to float across your imaginary movie screen.

Step seven: Remember the images you have seen, and the feelings or impressions they bring, so you can write them down and interpret them.

Pepper made herself comfortable on the seat and closed her eyes. She lifted one leg and relaxed it. She lifted the other leg and relaxed it. She lifted an arm.

"What are you doing?"

Pepper opened her eyes. Everett was staring at her. "Developing my ESP powers," Pepper replied.

"ESP?" Everett scoffed. "That's a bunch of baloney."

"No, it's not. Look at this book."

"Where'd you get that?"

"I found it."

"Let me see."

"No. I'm still reading it. When I'm finished I'm going to be able to read people's minds and make things move just by looking at them."

"Mental telepathy and telekinesis are two different things, in case you want to know."

"So? I'm going to learn how to do them both. Just watch."

Everett shrugged. "They're *both* a bunch of baloney," he said and returned to his *Popular Science*.

Outside the bus window the landscape had changed. There were more trees. The terrain had become hilly. Pepper tried to read her book, but now that the road had more twists and turns, her stomach knotted with motion sickness. She looked out the window, waiting for her stomach to settle. Her eyes began to droop.

Suddenly she was standing in front of a chain-link fence. On the other side was a dense green forest. She breathed in deeply. The rich, Christmassy smell of evergreens filled her nose. Oh, how she yearned to be in that forest! She clenched the metal fence so tightly her hands hurt. Then she let go. She rubbed her hands over her skull. And all she could feel was stubble.

Pepper woke with a start. Her heart was pounding. Her hands flew to her head, and she grabbed her thick curly hair with relief. It was only a dream, she told herself. But what a strange dream. It had felt so real. And the smell of the forest lingered in the air. Through the bus window she saw they were now deep in the mountains, skirting a sapphire-blue lake. Snow-capped mountain peaks were reflected in the water. There were tall evergreens all around—that must have been what triggered her dream.

Then she noticed her hands. On each palm she saw a criss-crossing of reddened lines. Almost as if she'd been grasping a chain-link fence.

But no! That couldn't be. Pepper rubbed both hands briskly against her thighs and looked again. The lines on her hands now seemed, as far as she could remember, to be the same lines she'd had all her life.

19

She straightened up in her seat and made herself take a couple of deep breaths to clear her head. Gradually she started to feel calm again.

She turned to Everett. "How long was I sleeping?"

"What?" Everett dragged his eyes away from his *Popular Science* magazine and looked at her blankly. "Were you sleeping?"

Pepper sighed loudly. She tucked the ESP book away in her duffel bag and pulled out her apple. As she was munching on it, something occurred to her. "Everett?"

Everett rattled his magazine to remind Pepper he was reading.

Pepper was not put off. "How come you get to keep all the money?"

"Because I'm the oldest. I'm responsible."

"I'm responsible too. Besides, some of it's for me. You should let me keep my own money."

"You'll spend it."

"No, I won't. I'll look after it. Promise."

"Fine! I'll give it to you if you'll stop bugging me." He dug down into his bag and pulled out several envelopes. One of them was marked "bus fare for trip home" in their mother's writing. He opened it, counted out half the bills, and handed the envelope to Pepper. "Here you go. But don't come crying to me if you lose it."

Pepper made a face. She stuck the envelope down into the very bottom of her duffel bag. She was not going to lose that money no matter what. She'd show him she was old enough and responsible enough to look after the money, and herself.

The bus trip felt endless. There were a couple of stops along the way, where they could get off the bus and use the bathroom. At the suppertime bus stop Everett bought them hot dogs and french fries and root beer. They only had twenty minutes, so Pepper gobbled her food and ran back to the bus as the big engine started up again. As the day wore on, the sinking sun played peekaboo behind the mountaintops. Shadows deepened and spread, the night gradually descending until the bus was blanketed in darkness.

Pepper slept fitfully through the night. When the dove-grey morning dawned they were approaching the outskirts of Vancouver. Outside the window she watched warehouses and billboards, rows of houses, and stores pass by. And then they were downtown, high-rise buildings all around. The bus rumbled through the city streets and finally pulled in to the bus terminal.

Pepper picked up her duffel bag and stepped off the bus. Her joints felt stiff, her muscles ached, and she was glad to leave the bus behind. The man at the ticket booth said they would have to wait several hours until the next bus left for the ferry. The waiting room had wooden benches, worn, dirty floors, and metal lockers along the walls. It smelled of dust and bleach, with an underlying whiff of urine.

"We could put our duffel bags in a locker and go out and look around the city," suggested Pepper.

"No," said Everett. "We better stay here. We don't want to get lost and miss our bus. You sit down and watch our stuff. I'll get us something for breakfast at the snack stand."

"Just 'cause you're older doesn't mean you get to decide everything, you know."

"Yes, it does."

Pepper scowled as she plopped down on the bench. Everett was a big stick-in-the-mud, she thought. No fun at all. She thought again about the kind of brother she wished she had. *That* brother would hire a taxi to drive them around the city and show them the sights. Or, better yet, they'd rent a hot-air balloon so they could float high over Vancouver, with snow-capped mountains on one side of them and the wide, blue ocean on the other.

On the bench across from her sat a man with a crooked nose and tattoos on his arms. He was smoking a cigarette. Pepper studied him discreetly. His pants were frayed at the hem. His suitcase was tied together with rope. Pepper quickly made up a story about him—just out of prison with only a bus ticket and loose change in his pocket. Maybe a switchblade knife too.

The man caught her looking at him. "Hey, kid," he said. He took a long draw on his cigarette. "Where you going?"

Pepper pretended not to hear. She hugged her duffel bag with the bus money in it a little closer.

The man chuckled. "There's nothing to be scared of. I'm just making some conversation to pass the time."

Pepper glanced nervously over at the snack stand. What was taking Everett so long? She could see him at the cash register counting out some change.

"Is that your brother?" asked the man, following her gaze.

Pepper nodded.

"He doesn't look like you."

Of course not, Pepper wanted to say. That's because he's not my real brother. But she didn't say a word. She hugged the duffel bag even closer and shifted uncomfortably on the bench.

Everett came back with two ham sandwiches.

"Let's sit over there," said Pepper, and they moved to the other side of the room.

Pepper shivered. She wasn't cold, but she felt like she was shaking off the encounter with the man the way a dog shakes rain from its fur. She had to admit it had been exciting talking to a possible ex-convict, one who may very well have been a kidnapper. In fact, the longer Pepper thought about it, the more she convinced herself she had only narrowly escaped being kidnapped herself.

CHAPTER 3

The Middle of Nowhere

Three hours later the bus pulled out of the terminal. When they finally boarded the ferry, Pepper and Everett took their bags up to the passenger lounge and sat by the windows, where they could see the bright blue water glittering with sunlight. Pepper made her way to the outside deck and ran up and down. It felt good to move her legs and finally be able to breathe fresh air. The wind buffeted her and the seagulls reeled and squawked overhead. She tapped on the window where she could see Everett sitting inside. Even though she was certain he must have heard her, he didn't look up from his magazine.

Pepper found a spot to sit on the deck, opened her ESP book, and turned to Chapter VII, The Mystery of Dream Impressions. She read that sleep is a special state in which the mind becomes very receptive. One sentence in particular caught her eye. "*The mind of every person with whom you are related, in any capacity, has thoughts about you and an inter-*

change of your thoughts with his is taking place on Subconscious levels, even while you sleep." Pepper considered this. What exactly did it mean? Was she actually making connections already with someone she was related to? She skimmed a bit more. *"You are living in two worlds at the same time—an outer world and an inner world. Your Subconscious Mind never sleeps. An intelligence within you is standing guard, day and night."* Pepper felt certain she was capable of tapping into that inner world—she just knew it. Now if she could only figure out how.

When the ferry arrived in Nanaimo, they spotted Grandma next to her dusty-blue Rambler, waving her arms over her head.

"Yoo hoo … Pepper … Everett … over here!" Grandma called. She was wearing a long, striped skirt, a polka-dotted top, a ratty old straw hat, and running shoes with holes cut out for her bunions.

Pepper took one look at the outfit and cringed. Her grandmother looked like a colour-blind hobo who had dressed in the dark. Pepper hoped that the other disembarking passengers wouldn't notice the strange getup, but Grandma kept drawing attention to herself, waving and calling out.

"Let me give you both a big hug." Pepper felt Grandma's arms around her. She smelled of salt and the sea. "How was your trip?" Grandma asked.

"Okay. Long, but okay."

Grandma hugged Everett next. "You're both growing up so fast," she said. "It seems like only yesterday that I was changing your diapers."

Everett turned such a bright red it was all Pepper could do to swallow a pig-snort laugh. The effort produced a strange gulping sound instead. When Grandma looked at her in surprise, it made her want to laugh all the more.

"Sorry," Pepper said, trying to wave away the feeling. Her eyes welled up as she struggled not to laugh. "Something caught in my throat."

"Do you want a lozenge? I think I've got one in here somewhere." Grandma began digging around in her purse. "Oh, here we go." She offered Pepper a hard green candy wrapped in cellophane. There were bits of lint stuck to it. It looked like it had been in the purse for years.

"No, thanks. I'm fine now."

"Everett?"

"No, thank you."

Grandma shrugged, unwrapped the candy, and popped it in her own mouth. "Well, throw your luggage in the trunk, and hop in."

Everett climbed into the front passenger seat, and Pepper jumped in the back.

As they drove north out of town, Grandma talked away. "It's about time you got to spend a summer with me on Shack Island. I love painting there. The light is incredible. Like no other place I can think of. It's almost magical." She glanced at Pepper in the rear-view mirror. "Are you excited?"

"Uh-huh," said Pepper, to be polite.

Grandma turned around to look directly at her. The car slid onto the gravel shoulder as it approached a corner.

"Watch the road!" yelled Pepper.

Grandma twisted around and yanked the steering wheel sharply, and the car veered back onto the pavement. She glanced over at Everett, then in the mirror at Pepper, and chuckled. "See that? My reflexes are still sharp as a tack." She brushed off the incident with a casual wave of the hand.

Pepper's stomach was feeling a bit woozy. She rolled down her window as Grandma's Rambler turned off the main road onto a smaller, winding road that hugged the shoreline. Pepper could see glimpses of the ocean between the trees.

"We're almost there now," Grandma said a few minutes later. "This is our road." She didn't use her indicator light as she swerved onto a narrow dirt road. The salal bushes on either side were coated white with dust. The car angled under some tall maple trees, nosed between a station wagon and a Volkswagen van, and stopped with a jerk.

"Shack Island," Grandma announced. "Three islands, really, but we call the whole place Shack Island."

Pepper peered through the windshield at three tiny islands a short distance from shore. The largest one was the closest. Clusters of ramshackle buildings dotted its shore. Some of them were painted in weather-worn reds and greens. Some were not painted at all. They were grouped higgledy-piggledy against the rocky bluffs.

Pepper and Everett glanced at each other silently. *This* was where they were going to spend the summer? They had not been expecting *real* shacks on Shack Island.

"But … they all look so old! They look like they're about to fall down," Pepper burst out.

"That's because they *are* old," Grandma said cheerfully. "Some are old fishermen's shacks. Been here for ages. Some were built back in the Depression, when times were hard. People built shacks to live in because they couldn't afford to pay their taxes. When I was a young girl, my family leased a bit of the land and put up a shack for a summer place. I've been coming here my whole life. A lot of the other families have been doing that too. Coming here every summer." Grandma paused, smiling as she remembered. Then her smile faded. "Things are changing around here, though. Progress, they call it. You used to find summer cabins in all the bays and coves along the coast road. Now what do you see? The cabins are disappearing. Big houses going up. More and more roads. More traffic." Grandma shook her head sadly. "But on Shack Island life has stayed simple. That's what makes it special."

Pepper stared at the shacks. They didn't look too special to her. She bit her tongue to stop herself from saying it out loud.

Grandma kept right on talking. "I hope it never changes, either. A while ago a bigwig land developer came up with a scheme to bulldoze the shacks and build fancy houses and marinas and such. But we all got together, everyone who lives here, and we fought against it. We stood up for what we believe in. There was a big protest, with signs and placards and petitions. And we stopped the developers. Now Shack Island can stay the way it's always been. Aren't we lucky?"

"Um … yes. I guess so," Pepper made herself say.

"See that area over there?" Grandma indicated a wide lagoon to the right. "That's Piper's Lagoon. You wouldn't believe it to look at it now, but at low tide the water goes out and all that's left is sand." Grandma slid the car key on top of the sun visor and started to get out of the car.

"Are you going to leave your key there?" Pepper asked.

"Sure. I always do. I never lose it that way."

"But aren't you afraid someone might steal the car?"

"Steal it? Of course not. This is Shack Island, not the big city." Grandma eased herself the rest of the way out of the car and opened the trunk. Pepper and Everett helped haul the luggage, bags of groceries, and several big glass bottles full of water down to the shore. Grandma had stashed her rowboat against the bank, well above the high-tide mark. Pepper wondered how everything was going to fit in one small boat.

"I'll grab this side. You two grab that side, and we'll carry it down to the water. Try not to let it drag on the rocks or it'll scrape the paint off," Grandma instructed.

They set the boat into the lapping waves and loaded it up. Grandma sat in the middle with the oars. Pepper threw her duffel bag and shoes into the bow, splashed through the water in her bare feet—the water brisk and refreshing against her hot, travel-dusty skin—and climbed in.

When Everett heaved in his duffel bag, the boat rocked.

"What've you got in there? Bricks?" asked Grandma.

"No. Books. Magazines. *Popular Science.*"

"Well, I hope you're not going to spend your summer inside reading. You'll want to get out and swim and fish. Meet some of the other kids on the island. There's another boy, Barry Brewster, just a few doors down. I bet you and Barry will hit it off."

Everett didn't respond. Pepper saw his jaw tighten. Making friends wasn't one of Everett's strong points. He was more of a loner.

"All right, let's head off. Give the boat a good shove, Everett, and jump in," Grandma said.

Everett did as he was told, climbing awkwardly into the boat. Grandma pulled on the oars and they bobbed across the water. As they approached the main island, Pepper had a better view of the ragtag shacks. They'd been built close together, with hardly room to walk between them. The rooflines pitched this way and that, as if the shacks had been tossed ashore in a storm. Porches seemed to be attached precariously with bits of driftwood and rope, sloping where they should be straight. A jaunty flag fluttered from a crooked pole. Lines of laundry danced in the breeze. Someone waved to them and Grandma waved back.

Pepper trailed her fingers in the cool, clear water. The sun glanced brightly off the ripples her fingers left on the surface. What word had Grandma used to describe the light here? Magical. Pepper thought she could understand now what Grandma had meant. She looked into the darkening depths. She could catch glimpses of rocks in the watery shadows and flowing seaweed. A big purple starfish. What other mysterious treasures lay hidden out of sight?

The boat rounded a rocky bluff and came upon a crescent beach. Here, again, another sprouting of jumbled shacks and lean-tos. Each one was cobbled together—a rickety set of stairs here, a patched roof there.

"That's my place, my painting shack." Grandma pointed to a weather-beaten shack snuggled up in the lee of the bluff. "I call it the Periwinkle."

Pepper eyed it dubiously. All she could hope was that it would look better on the inside than it did on the outside. "What's a periwinkle?" she asked.

"It's a tiny little animal that lives in a shell. It looks like a snail, but it's only about the size of your little fingernail. You'll see them on the beach and in tidal pools."

Good name for a tiny little shack, thought Pepper. Although if she was naming it, she would call it The Horrible Hovel, or maybe The Shack of Banishment, or even The Middle of Nowhere.

An old man in overalls came down to the water's edge

to meet them. He grabbed the bow of the boat and held it steady. "Hi there, Evelyn. These your grandkids?"

"They sure are, Bus. This is Pepper. And this is Everett."

Bus grinned. One of his front teeth was missing. "You've got your boat filled to the gills today!"

"You can say that again. Even so, I only got half my groceries. I wanted to make sure I had enough room for Pepper and Everett and all their luggage. In a couple of days I'll go back into town and get the rest of my groceries."

Bus helped them toss their gear onto the beach and carry the boat up beside the shack.

Grandma led the way up the crooked steps. Above the door a piece of driftwood had been nailed in place. *The Periwinkle*, it read, each letter a different colour. Two snail-like shells had been painted at either end. The door angled off-kilter as Grandma pushed it open.

She stepped aside, waving them in. "Come on in. Make yourselves at home. It's rustic, but it has everything we need."

Pepper stopped in the doorway. It was the tiniest house she had ever seen, not much bigger than a garden shed. She wanted to turn around and go straight back home again.

Not only was the Periwinkle small, it was crowded. There was a wood stove in the middle of the room. A table and three mismatched chairs were arranged under a window that looked out over the bay. Shelves of cans and Grandma's homemade preserves lined one wall. Another shelf over the counter held pots and pans and dishes. Grandma's easel and paints were set up in a corner, with canvases in various stages of completion stacked up against the wall. On the far side of the room a heavy wire had been strung through eyelets screwed into the ceiling. It held some purple paisley curtains that hung from ceiling to floor. Grandma pushed aside the curtain at the back.

"This is where I sleep," she said. "It doesn't get the light." A narrow cot was set up against the wall. "I thought Everett could have the one beside it. It has a shelf for his science magazines." She pulled open the middle curtain. This alcove, too, had a narrow bed, and a flimsy bookshelf made of planks and bricks. "And the one at the front can be Pepper's."

Pepper pulled back her curtain. Her space was the only one with a window. The window was propped open and a salty breeze stirred the air. A fine mesh screen had been tacked over the opening to keep the bugs out. The bed was pushed right up under the window.

Pepper threw herself full length onto the bed, making the springs creak in protest. The blanket smelled of mustiness and mothballs. She stretched her arms up over her head. From where she lay she could see the sky and a wispy cotton-ball cloud. She could hear the wash of the waves against the beach. If she'd been in a better frame of mind, she might have appreciated these things. But not today.

She turned on her side to study her bedroom—if it could be called a bedroom. It didn't even have proper walls. It was so small she could almost reach out and touch the faded purple curtain that separated her room from Everett's next door. She could hear him moving around, unpacking his gear.

The floorboards of her room were rough and splintery. A makeshift side table (to be more precise, an apple crate) was wedged between the bed and the curtain. She poked her head inside it, and a surprised spider scurried into a dark corner.

And to think she used to complain about the attic room

at home, Pepper thought bitterly as she grabbed her duffel bag and dumped the contents onto her bed. She poked the spider out of the apple crate, stuffed her clothes inside, and kicked her runners under the bed. The ESP book found a place on the top of the apple crate, along with her writing paper and pen. The last item was the envelope with the bus money. She slid it carefully, out of sight, behind the apple crate. In less than a minute she had unpacked.

Pepper sat down on the creaky bed and let out a groan. It was going to be a long, long summer.

Her gaze fell on the pen on top of the apple crate. She could write a letter and tell her mom and dad she wanted to come home right away. But, on second thought, what would be the point? They wouldn't care. They wanted her out of the way. In fact, maybe she wouldn't write to them all summer. That would serve them right.

Pepper was still staring at the pen when a thrilling idea popped into her head. She rubbed her hands together and tucked them under her legs, then concentrated her attention on the pen. She narrowed her eyes, determined to make the pen move with the power of her mind. Move, she thought as hard as she could. Move! She imagined how it would happen. First the pen would wobble slightly, almost imperceptibly. Then it would start a definite rocking, side to side, and there would be no doubt that her powers were working. Finally the pen would break into a satisfying roll across the top of the apple crate and drop to the floor. She could do it. She knew she could. She stared at the pen so hard it seemed to blur, multiplying into two pens. She felt certain she was on the verge of making it move.

"What do you think?" Grandma poked her head around the curtain, breaking Pepper's concentration.

"About the pen?"

"The pen? No. Your room."

"Oh. I guess it will be okay." It was hard to keep the annoyance out of her voice. Was there *no* privacy here? She glanced at the pen, which remained stubbornly still, and then back at Grandma, whose bright expression had faded slightly.

"I mean, great," Pepper said. "Just great."

The smile returned to Grandma's face. "I'm so glad you like it. When you're finished unpacking, we can have a snack." The curtain fell back into place.

After Pepper and Everett had finished their biscuits and milk, things got worse.

"Where's the bathroom?" Pepper asked.

"There's no bathroom," Grandma replied.

"What?" Pepper and Everett both said together.

"There's an outhouse in the back."

Pepper was aghast. "You're kidding!"

Grandma stood up and calmly began clearing away the glasses. "I'm not kidding, Pepper. No one has a bathroom on this island. Only outhouses. There's no running water here. It's like camping, but without a tent."

Pepper crossed her arms. She could feel her expression turn sour. "No shower?"

"No. And no bath either. I go into town every week or two. You can bathe then. Or you can go swimming to get clean. We have to conserve the water we have. The water in the glass bottles is for drinking, and the water from the rain barrel outside is for washing the dishes." These inconveniences did not seem to bother Grandma at all. She continued. "There's no electricity. And no phone either."

Pepper grimaced. "So, no TV?"

"No TV."

"How about when it gets dark? What do we do for light?"

"Lanterns." Grandma indicated a hurricane lantern hanging on a nail by the door. "And I've got a flashlight. Candles too."

Everett piped up. "You could get a generator."

Grandma just smiled.

Everett pressed on. "You could make your own electricity with a generator."

Grandma put her hands on her hips. "Everett, if I wanted a place with electricity I would have stayed in town, wouldn't I?"

Pepper wished they *were* staying in town, but she bit her tongue and said instead, "All right. Can you tell me where the outhouse is, please?"

"Out back. You can't miss it."

The outhouse was no bigger than an upended travelling trunk. It was covered in shingles and leaned to one side. Pepper pulled open the door. All it contained was a wooden seat with a hole cut in the middle, and a roll of toilet paper in the corner. She wrinkled her nose at the smell, pulled the door closed behind her, and secured it with the hook. As she sat in the outhouse, she pondered her predicament. No phone. No TV. No electricity. No indoor plumbing. A fine summer this was turning out to be!

At that moment, when Pepper thought things couldn't possibly get any worse, two mosquitoes landed on her at the same time. One bit her on the ankle, and the other on her arm.

After supper Grandma sat down to write up her to-do list for the next day. "I have to write everything down, or I won't remember it. When I'm working on my paintings, I get so immersed in the process I forget about everything else. I'm thinking about the light and the shade, and the colours, and the mood I'm going for. Even when I'm not actually painting, I'm looking at a painting, or thinking about it. Hours and hours can go by before I even realize. So I make lists for everything. Lists for groceries. Lists of things to do when I go into town. Lists of things to remember to tell people. Lists of all my lists." She stood up. "Okay. What's next?" She checked the list. "Wash the dishes."

Grandma showed Pepper how to fill a plastic tub with water from the rain barrel outside, and then she dumped the dirty supper dishes in.

"You wash the dishes in cold water?"

"Yes. Most of the time I do. But if it's cold outside, and I have the wood stove on, I'll heat the water up." She handed Pepper a dishtowel. "I'll wash. You dry."

For the first few minutes Pepper dried in silence. Then she said, "Grandma, if we don't have a phone, how are we going to know when the baby is born?"

Grandma smiled. "Don't worry. I have friends your parents can phone, and they'll come right over and let us know as soon as they hear anything."

Pepper picked up another plate and dried it slowly. "Grandma, do you know anything about my real family?"

"Your real family?"

"You know ... my *real* family. The family I was born into, before I was adopted."

Grandma shrugged. "There's not a lot to tell. It was such a long time ago."

"But you must remember something."

"Let's see ... I remember the day your mom and dad

brought you home. We all thought you were such a lovely child. Curly hair. Rosy cheeks. You were the girl they'd been wishing for."

Yeah, right, thought Pepper. Until they found out they were expecting a new baby. "But what else?"

"Nothing, really. The orphanage doesn't give any information from before. It's a fresh start when you're adopted."

Pepper considered this. Then she asked, "You saw me the day they brought me home?"

"I sure did."

"Back home? You were there? Visiting us?"

"No. Here. Here in Nanaimo. It was before you all moved to the Prairies. Just before your dad's company transferred him there."

This came as a surprise to Pepper. She'd always assumed she was born and adopted back home. But she'd been born in Nanaimo. Somewhere here, twelve, almost thirteen years ago, her life had begun. It was a bit unsettling thinking she'd been wrong all this time about the very place where she'd been born.

Pepper put the last dish away. She waited to hear more about the adoption, but Grandma didn't say another word. Pepper had a strange feeling Grandma knew more of the story than she was letting on.

As Pepper hung up the dishtowel, she glanced at Grandma's to-do list still sitting on the counter. One item caught her eye. "Tell Pepper about the Fergusons." An idea popped into Pepper's head and her heart skipped a beat. "Grandma, who are the Fergusons?"

"The Fergusons?" Grandma looked puzzled.

"Yes. The Fergusons. Right here." Pepper pointed to the item.

37

Grandma put on her reading glasses and looked at the list. "Oh! The Fergusons are the people your parents will phone when the baby is born. I wanted to make sure I remembered to tell you."

Pepper thought she caught a hint of secrecy in Grandma's expression. Then her grandmother smiled and started humming to herself. Pepper watched Grandma's behaviour closely. She thought she looked exactly like someone pretending she had nothing to hide.

CHAPTER 4

Picnic at Ghost Island

Pepper woke the next morning to the sounds of seagulls hopping around on the roof. She sat up and looked out the window. The sea was brilliant blue. Sunlight sparkled off the water. The air had a brightness to it, as if a handful of glitter had been tossed up in the sky. A fresh breeze pushed through the screen.

It was chilly in the little shack. Pepper dressed quickly—bathing suit, plaid pedal-pushers, and a sweatshirt—and then shoved her feet into her runners. She dragged a comb through her tangled hair and pulled a hair band into place. There was no mirror to check to see how she looked.

Grandma was already awake. "Morning," she said as she lit the wood stove and put the kettle on. "Did you sleep well?"

"My mosquito bites were itchy at first—but then I had a really sound sleep. It's so quiet here at night."

Grandma set a bowl of cereal on the table in front

of Pepper. "What time does Everett usually get up?" she asked.

"He likes to sleep in. He goes to bed late and gets up late." She'd heard his transistor radio playing quietly into the night as she'd lain awake wondering about her real family.

"So he's a night owl," Grandma said. "Not me. Early to bed and early to rise." She poured herself a cup of tea. "I'm going to have a morning dip. Do you want to join me?"

Pepper shook her head as she wolfed down her cereal. She couldn't imagine rising from a warm, cozy bed and plunging directly into the icy sea. "Maybe later. I thought I'd look around the island this morning."

"All right, then. Just keep an eye on the tides. There's a low tide in the middle of the day today. You can walk to each island when it's at its lowest, and over to Piper's Lagoon as well. You can even walk over to where we've parked the car. But remember that the tide will start to come up again before too long. You don't want to be stranded on the other side. Make sure you're back on this island by two o'clock."

"Okay. I'll remember."

"Maybe you should take something to eat. What would you like? Crackers and cheese? A sandwich?"

"I'll just take an apple." Pepper picked the shiniest, reddest one from the bowl on the table and bounced down the crooked stairs. The air smelled of seaweed and salt and rotting wood. Clumps of long yellow grass sprouted from the rocky ground. The wind rushed this way and that through the grass, whisking it in circles. Well-worn paths had been beaten through the grass. Behind the outhouse a few beached logs were lodged in the gravel at the high-tide mark. This side of the island faced south, towards Piper's Lagoon. Pepper jumped from one log to the next, munching on her apple as she went. The bark on the logs had been broken off, exposing the sun-bleached wood below. Bits of seaweed, shells, and debris had washed up and been trapped between the logs. Overhead a seagull soared in the wind like a kite.

Pepper noticed a girl farther down the beach walking in her direction. The girl appeared to be about Pepper's age, maybe a little older. As she got closer, Pepper could see that the girl wore her light brown hair in a pixie cut and had on blue terry cloth shorts and a short top that revealed a tanned midriff. These kinds of tops were the latest style, but naturally Pepper didn't have one.

The girl looked Pepper up and down, pausing for a second as she took in Pepper's plaid pedal-pushers. "Hi," she said. "I'm Chloe."

"I'm Pepper."

"Pepper?"

"Yeah. My real name's Allison, but everyone calls me Pepper."

"How come?"

People always asked the same question. Pepper was used to it. "'Cause of my red hair. You know, like a red pepper."

"Oh, I get it. Are you staying for the summer?"

Pepper nodded. "Are you?"

"Yup. My family has one of the shacks on the other side of the bluff. We come here every summer. You're staying at the Periwinkle, right?"

"How'd you know that?"

Chloe laughed. "Everybody on this island knows everybody else's business. My mom says if you sneeze, someone in the next shack will say 'Bless you.' I saw you come over in your grandma's boat yesterday."

"She's not my real grandma."

"She's not?"

"No. I'm adopted."

"Really?" Chloe's eyes widened. "I've never met anyone who's adopted before. What's it like being adopted?"

Pepper shrugged.

Chloe persisted. "Do you ever wonder about your real family? I mean … not knowing where you came from? I'd want to know that, right off the bat. And then the whole bit about living with someone else's family. That would seem kind of … well, weird to me."

"Yeah. I guess it is sometimes," admitted Pepper.

Chloe kept staring at her, but when Pepper didn't elaborate she said, "Hey, do you want me to show you around the islands?"

"Sure. Okay," said Pepper, glad the topic had changed.

Chloe led the way between the shacks towards the beach on the other side. They passed a clothesline with a beach towel and a rigid-looking woman's bathing suit, still dripping wet. It was constructed with numerous complicated panels. The seams appeared to be reinforced with heavy wires. The flowery pattern looked like something you might see curtains made out of, or a couch. Beside it hung a rubber bathing cap covered in plastic flowers and sporting a chinstrap.

"Eww. Who'd wear that?" said Pepper with a pig-like snort. The snort turned into a full-blown laugh and Chloe began to laugh along.

Then Chloe said, "It's your grandma's. I've seen her swimming in it."

"No!" Pepper stopped laughing. She was mortified. Of course it would end up being Grandma's bathing suit and gaudy bathing cap. Why did everything about her family have to be so embarrassing?

They reached the north-facing beach a few minutes later. The wind blew stronger on this side of the island. Behind them the shacks crowded together along the flat spine of the island. Some had smoke curling out of the chimneys, obviously occupied. Others were boarded up.

"How many people live here?" asked Pepper.

Chloe shrugged. "It's hard to say. People come and go. Usually there are people living in about half of the shacks. Just for the summer, though. The rest of the year there's no one here. The whole place is deserted. See that white one that looks like a boathouse?" Chloe pointed to a flat-fronted building with a set of wooden runners leading down to the beach like train tracks. "That's where Barry Brewster lives. He thinks he knows everything. The one next to it is where Bus lives."

Pepper nodded. "I met Bus yesterday. He helped us carry the boat up to the cabin."

"He's a nice guy, one of the old-timers. He built that raft anchored out there in the bay for the kids," Chloe said. "Come on. I'll show you where I live. It's just my mom and me during the week. My dad stays in town 'cause he has to work. He only comes out on the weekends." She led the way up a set of stairs at the base of the bluff. The stairs were rough and ladder-like and petered out almost before they started. From there a path of beaten-down grass snaked higher and higher through scraggy oak trees.

"Careful here." Chloe pointed to a patch of thistles. "They're prickly."

When they reached the top they turned around to look at the view. The row of shacks stretched out below, one after the other, a hodgepodge of rooflines. The island was narrow and windblown, a beach on either side. The two smaller Shack Islands were not much farther out, and beyond that, a huge expanse of ocean stretched for miles and miles, all the way to the mountains of the mainland. A tiny tugboat pulled a massive log boom slowly across the water. Pepper could hear the thump-thump-thump of the engine, low-pitched like a heartbeat. She liked the ruggedness of the rocky coastline, the way the sea-gulls soared overhead, and the smell of salt in the air. It was so different from the flat prairie landscape she was used to.

"Watch your step going down here. It's pretty steep," said Chloe as she climbed down the other side of the bluff to a green shack with a veranda all along the front. Stilts supported one end of the building where the rocks dipped away.

Chloe's mom looked up from reading a *Chatelaine* magazine. She was sitting on a wicker chair on the veranda. Her hair was in metal rollers.

"Mom, this is Pepper," said Chloe. "She's staying with her grandma in the Periwinkle."

"Hello, Pepper. Evelyn told me she was expecting her grandkids."

"Could we get some lunch?" asked Chloe.

Her mom looked at her watch. "Don't tell me you're hungry already. You just had your breakfast."

"I want to pack a picnic. I'm showing Pepper around."

"There's Velveeta cheese in the cooler. You can make sandwiches. And remember, don't go talking to those hippies over on Middle Island."

As Chloe wrapped the sandwiches in wax paper and put

them in a bag, she whispered under her breath, "I hate how my mom still treats me like a kid."

"Well, we are kids," Pepper whispered back.

"Not me. I'm a teenager now."

When they climbed up the bluff and into the gusting wind again, they could see that the tide had gone out noticeably in the short time they'd been at Chloe's cabin. A skinny tract of land had emerged from the water to connect one of the smaller Shack Islands to the main island. It reminded Pepper of a thin stalk supporting a piece of fruit.

"Look," Pepper shouted against the wind. "We can walk over to that island now."

Chloe turned to shout back. "That's Middle Island. I'll take you over there first. When the tide goes out a little farther, we'll be able to walk to the other island too." Her pixie cut was dancing around her head, blown first in one direction and then another.

It seemed strange to Pepper that this family of islands could actually be linked together. Deep down, they were connected. Most of the time you just couldn't see it.

The two girls scrambled like mountain goats down the precipitous path. Once they reached the shacks the ground flattened out and the walking became easier. The rocks were still wet where the tide had retreated, and it took them only a few minutes to cross over to Middle Island. It was much smaller than the main island, with steep rocky cliffs and only a few shacks stuck like barnacles around its perimeter.

"The Englishes live in the first shack. And see that one?" Chloe was pointing to a shack where wind chimes tinkled on the porch and multicoloured tie-dyed curtains hung in the windows. "That's where the hippies live. They're renting it for the summer. Mom thinks they're draft dodgers from the States."

"What are draft dodgers?"

"Well … Mom says the United States is fighting a war in a country called Vietnam. Boys can get called up to be soldiers when they turn nineteen. But some of them don't want to fight in the war. They come up here to Canada instead so they don't have to go to war. People call them draft dodgers."

Pepper noticed a big peace sign hanging on the shack's front door. She'd seen hippies back home wearing the same symbol on necklaces and T-shirts.

"Why doesn't your mom like draft dodgers?"

"She says people should be proud to fight for their country. My dad thinks the same way. He fought in the Second World War, back before we were born. He's a war hero. He got a medal and everything. When he came back from the war, there was a big parade for the troops and the whole town came out and cheered for them. My dad says they were brave men back then, not cowards. Draft dodgers are just a bunch of hippies. None of them work, and they sit around smoking marijuana all day long."

"Marijuana?"

"You know. It's a drug. Haven't you ever heard of marijuana? You smoke it like a cigarette."

"I know that," Pepper said, although she didn't know much about it at all. "How do you know they're not smoking regular cigarettes?"

"Mom says you can tell by the way it smells."

As they walked by the shack, Pepper thought she caught a whiff of smoke, but it smelled like an ordinary campfire.

The shoreline on the near side of the island was easy to walk along, but when they reached the point it became almost impassable. They turned back the way they had come. By that time the tide had gone out far enough they could walk to the third island.

"We call this one Ghost Island," Chloe explained. "It's the smallest of the islands. Some people say it's haunted."

Pepper studied the small rocky outcropping. Windblown brush and stunted trees clung to the island. A solitary olive-coloured cabin, all boarded up, was built against the rocks. "Does anyone live there?"

"Not right now. Usually there is. I guess they'll come later in the summer."

"Is it really haunted?"

"That's the story. People say it's a ghost who's waiting for a fisherman to return from sea. But the fisherman was lost in a storm years and years ago. And the ghost is still waiting. Some nights people say they hear a wailing sound. Some say it's just the wind. But my dad heard it one time, and he swears it was a human voice."

Pepper shivered. She could imagine how terrified she'd be if she heard a wailing ghost in the night.

As they talked, the two girls trudged across the gravelly beach towards the island. There was a definite eeriness about the place. A crow huddled on a craggy branch of an oak tree, watching their approach. The wind blew harder here, more insistently. It raced through the gnarly trees. And it circled around Pepper, buffeting her this way and that like a bad-tempered spirit. The sun ducked behind a passing cloud and the sky grew darker. Pepper felt uneasy. If it had been up to her, she would have turned around right then and gone back. But Chloe kept walking on ahead, chattering away as if everything was completely normal. Pepper steadied her nerves and made herself run a few steps to catch up.

Once they reached Ghost Island, the sun came out again. They walked along the shore, looking in tidal pools and jumping over starfish. Chloe pointed out sea anemones with beautiful orange feathery plumes, tiny periwinkles, and sea urchins bristling with spines. She stopped at a flat, table-height rock. "This is the picnic rock," she said, and she began to unpack the lunch bag.

Pepper stood a few steps away, completely still, staring off into the distance. She saw bright sunlight. Shimmering heat waves. Then a prickly sensation washed over her. An image began to take shape out of the glare of light. It was a girl with her back towards Pepper. She sat on a ragged patchwork quilt made of different fabrics, all sizes and colours. The girl ran her hand back and forth along the quilt as she gazed out towards the water. Then the girl turned suddenly, as if she'd heard a sound. She looked back over her shoulder in Pepper's direction.

Pepper blinked her eyes, and the image vanished. The girl on the quilt was gone. All that remained was the beach and the water. What had she seen? Some kind of mirage? A trick of the light? Or something otherworldly?

"What's with you?" Chloe said, turning around.

Pepper gave a start. "It's nothing. I just thought I saw something."

"What?"

"Nothing important." But the truth was Pepper felt more than a little shaken. Why had this strange image come out of nowhere? Was her mind playing tricks on her? Pepper ate the sandwich Chloe handed her, but she didn't feel hungry at all.

48

When they were finished, Chloe stood up and brushed off the crumbs. "We better get going before the tide comes in."

Pepper was glad to start moving again. She wanted to shake off the uneasiness the image of the strange girl had left her with.

Back at the main island, Chloe suggested they swim out to the raft in the bay. In a matter of seconds they stripped down to their bathing suits and rushed into the water. At first the cold, sea-slippery water was a shock to the skin. There was the salt-water sting on their mosquito bites, and then a delicious smoothness as the water wound ribbon-like around their bodies. When Pepper dove under, the only sound was a bubbling noise as she moved her limbs. Rocks glowed beneath her mysteriously in the murky light.

When Pepper surfaced, she pushed her hair off her fore-head and looked around. "Race you to the raft," she yelled. Pepper loved swimming, but back home she only got the chance if she went to the community pool. The girls splashed through the water and reached the raft at the same time. They paused to catch their breath before heaving themselves up onto it.

"This is a great place for tanning," said Chloe, stretching out full length. "I want to get a good tan this summer. When I go back to school, I'm going to have the best tan ever."

Chloe's body in its royal-blue two-piece bathing suit was long and lean, just beginning to take on the suggestion of a womanly shape. Pepper's own bathing suit was red. It was the same one-piece bathing suit she'd had for the past two years. She thought she looked like a giant jelly bean in it. She stretched out on the raft, stomach down, and laid her cheek on her crossed arms.

"You should let me put some makeup on you one day," said Chloe.

"What for?"

"It would make you look older. Cuter, too."

"What's wrong with the way I look now?"

Chloe put up her hands. "Okay, okay. I was just trying to help."

Several minutes of offended silence followed. Then Chloe said, "A dentist could fix that gap between your teeth, you know."

"So?"

"So why don't you ask your parents if you could do it?"

"Maybe I like it this way," said Pepper. She felt the space between her two front teeth with her tongue. It was such a part of her, it was hard to imagine it not being there. Especially if that meant wearing braces. "You know, Chloe, *some* people have more important things to think about than the way they look."

"Oh, I know. Do you think I should grow my hair out?"

Pepper didn't answer. As she looked across the rippling water towards the shacks, she saw Everett sitting by himself reading on the steps of the Periwinkle. Another boy was walking along the beach towards the shack. He was big and stocky, sporting a striped shirt and a brush cut. The boy stopped when he noticed Everett. Pepper was too far away to hear what he said, but by looking at them—the way Everett remained sitting, looking down, pretending to keep reading, the cocky way the other boy stood—she could tell what was happening. She had seen it before. Everett attracted bullies the way a horse attracts flies.

"That's Barry Brewster, the one I told you about, from the boathouse," said Chloe. She had propped herself up on her elbows and was watching too. Then she asked, "Is that your brother?"

"Yup."

"He's kinda cute."

"Barry?"

"No! Your brother."

"He is?"

"Sure. In kind of a serious way. Some girls go for that type."

As far as Pepper knew, no girl had ever shown even a passing interest in Everett.

"He doesn't look very strong, though," Chloe continued. "He wouldn't stand a chance if he got in a fight with Barry. Barry's a real fighter. Once he broke another guy's nose."

Pepper sat up. Barry was laughing now, and Everett had hunched down as if he wanted to disappear. Barry turned, still laughing, and sauntered off down the beach.

That evening Grandma made them hot chocolate, and then Pepper brushed her teeth and got into her pajamas. She pulled the covers up, turned on the flashlight, and opened her ESP book. She could hear Everett rustling around in the bedroom cubicle next to hers and was determined to read his mind. She reviewed the ESP steps one to seven. One to five were easy. The hard one was step number six. Try as she might, she saw no ESP images crossing the blank screen of her mind. Instead, she kept thinking about how itchy the mosquito bites on her ankle and arm were. She scratched them vigorously, then tried to practise her ESP skills on Grandma. She reread the steps just to make sure she was doing it right. She made her body relax completely. She made her mind go blank. And then she drifted off.

All of a sudden, Pepper felt her heart beating hard in her chest. She was outside, and it was nighttime. There was blackness all around. No street lights. She was running down a country road. Tall trees on either side. The stars glittered overhead in the cloudless sky. The Big Dipper loomed, magnificent and brilliant, tipped sideways at a rakish angle near the horizon. She was running towards it, straining to reach it. Her breath came in short puffs. Then a sound in the distance. Quiet at first but coming closer. A car! She looked over her shoulder and saw two pinpricks of light, then veered into the trees and crouched down out of sight until the lights passed. She waited. One, two, three seconds, and then back onto the road again. She looked up into the sky, but the Big Dipper was no longer there.

Pepper woke with a start. It was the middle of the night. She was covered in sweat. As she lay on her bed, waiting for the dream to fade, she gradually became aware of a tapping sound against the screen window. Was someone there? She sat bolt upright and looked out. The night was bathed in moonlight. A moth was outside, fluttering against the screen, trying to get in.

She lay down again. In the dark, she could hear the moth still bumping against the screen. She couldn't fall asleep again for a long time.

Just Imagine

"Who wants to go blackberry picking?" Grandma asked the following morning. "The first berries of the season should be ripening right about now. It's the wild ones I'm after. They're small, and they're hard to find, but they're worth the trouble."

Pepper looked up from her porridge. "Chloe and I went all over these islands, but we didn't see any."

"We have to cross over to the car park and go down the road. I know a couple of good places to look." Grandma picked up her green-covered tide book and scanned the columns. "The low tides are usually about twelve or thirteen hours apart. They get a little later each day. That's why it's good to check. Mmm … low tide today at one. If we time it right we can walk over and back again. We won't have to take the boat. We can pick up a quart of milk at the store while we're over there."

"There's a store around here?" Pepper asked.

"It's not a big one, but it has the basics. It's about a fifteen-minute walk farther down the road."

Grandma, Pepper, and Everett each carried a plastic ice cream pail as they trudged across the barnacled rocks and up the bank to the car park. They poked along the side of the road, pushing aside the prickly brambles to get deeper into the bushes, where Grandma said the best berries were. The vines spread over the ground like tattered lace. Grandma and Everett made frequent forays into the forest. The tall evergreens provided cool shade, but Pepper suspected there might be cougars hiding in the shadows. If she was a cougar, that was exactly the kind of place she'd lie in wait.

"Aren't you two afraid of cougars?" Pepper called to them.

"Cougars? Nonsense!" Grandma said. "I swear you have a more active imagination than anyone I know."

"The probability of encountering a cougar is extremely low," Everett chimed in. "Cougars prefer to avoid humans. Besides, their prime hunting times are dawn and dusk."

Pepper pulled a face. "Dawn and dusk," she mimicked under her breath. "Thank you very much, professor!" Even though she knew Everett was usually correct—annoyingly so—Pepper still decided she would stay close to the road. After half an hour, she was hot and sticky. Her arms and legs were scratched, and she'd eaten more berries than had ended up in the pail.

Pepper sat down in the tall grass and waited. The sun beat down. The air was heavy with the scent of wild-flowers and grasses. She heard some black seed pods on the broom bushes snapping open in the heat. A dragon-fly appeared, tick-tick-ticking as it circled lazily, rainbow winged. Meandering. Touching down briefly on a purple-crowned thistle and then taking flight again.

Just as Grandma and Everett emerged from the woods, a shiny silver car pulled over on the side of the road, and a man wearing sunglasses called out, "Hi, there, Evelyn. How are you today?"

Grandma walked over to the car. "Hello, Michael. I'm well, thank you. I've got my grandkids with me now. This is Pepper and Everett."

The man gave them a friendly smile.

As the two adults chatted, Pepper noticed how dowdy Grandma looked with her old-lady legs sticking out from baggy Bermuda shorts, her cut-away runners for bunions, and her straw hat tied on with a long striped scarf.

She heard the man say, "I'm heading home now. Why don't you three come around to the house? Marjorie would love to see you. April's home too."

"That would be lovely," said Grandma. "You go on ahead. We'll walk over that way."

The man waved as the silver car, sleek as a space rocket, roared off down the road.

"Who was that?" asked Pepper.

"Michael Ferguson. His wife, Marjorie, is a painter in my art group. Very talented. She mostly works in oils. They live in the big house on the point. They're the ones I told you about. Your mom and dad will phone them when the baby's born. They promised to come over and let us know as soon as they hear any news," Grandma said.

When Pepper heard the name Ferguson, she thought of her grandma's list: "Tell Pepper about the Fergusons." Was there something else Grandma had left unsaid?

Grandma peered into Pepper's ice cream pail. Only a few berries rolled around in the bottom. "Oh, dear. Is that all you picked?"

Pepper hoped there weren't too many berry stains around her mouth.

"Well, never mind," Grandma continued. "You'll get the knack of finding them. You have to know where to look. How did you manage, Everett?"

Everett had enough berries to cover several inches at the bottom of his pail.

"Good for you!" Grandma was pleased. "If we put them all together I think we'll have enough for a pie."

They set off down the road, turned onto a gravel side road, and eventually came to a pair of wrought-iron gates, standing open. The driveway cut through a thick green forest. Shafts of light slanted through the trees. A floor of pine and fir needles softened their footsteps. Mr. Ferguson's silver car was parked in front of an impressive stone house with massive timbers. Right beside it was a shiny red convertible.

Grandma banged the heavy brass-ring knocker on the enormous cedar door.

Michael Ferguson welcomed them in. He was a tall man, Pepper noted. Much taller than her own dad.

"Do you already have company? I see there's another car here," said Grandma.

"Oh, that's Marjorie's new car. I got it for her birthday. Isn't it a beauty?"

Pepper looked back at the gleaming cars. Two cars for one family! And one had been a birthday present. What luxury. Her dad had given her mom a toaster for her birthday.

Mr. Ferguson ushered them into a huge living room with a high ceiling and a stone fireplace that took up an entire wall. The far wall was all glass, and it looked out over a sky-blue swimming pool to the sea beyond.

"Wow," breathed Pepper.

A woman with strawberry-blonde hair, styled so it flipped up at the ends, came to meet them. "How nice to see you, Evelyn," she said.

Grandma made the introductions. "Marjorie, these are my grandkids, Pepper and Everett. We've got to go to the store and make it back before the tide turns, so we can't stay long."

"Well, come and sit down for a little while at least," Marjorie Ferguson said. "Would you like something cool to drink?"

Pepper sat on one of the big couches. It was so deep that when she settled back, her feet no longer touched the floor. She sipped the glass of pop Mrs. Ferguson brought her. It had ice cubes in it that clinked against the side of the glass. She studied the Fergusons as they talked to Grandma. They must be close to her parents' age, she guessed, but they seemed much younger. Mr. Ferguson wore crisply creased slacks and an expensive-looking pale yellow shirt. Mrs. Ferguson had a long, graceful neck like a ballerina's. Even the way she sat, with her legs crossed to the side, seemed elegant.

Mrs. Ferguson was talking about a trip their family had taken to California. "It was lovely to get away. And flying these days! It's so quick. We were just talking about going again, weren't we, Michael? Maybe in the fall."

"Oh, yes. Definitely."

Pepper leaned forward. "Did you see the sidewalk with all the stars in it?"

Mr. Ferguson nodded. "The Walk of Fame? We sure did."

"And palm trees, and the big Hollywood sign on the hills? And Disneyland?"

"Yes, yes, and yes." He grinned.

Pepper leaned back again. Just imagine, she thought. Imagine hopping on a plane whenever you felt like it. She finished her drink and set it down on a coaster on the side table. "Do you mind if I use your bathroom?" she asked.

"It's down the hall on the right," Mrs. Ferguson said.

The hallway was long with many doors leading off it. Pepper picked one door and opened it. It wasn't the bathroom. It was a teenage girl's bedroom. And it was exactly the bedroom she'd always dreamed of having. The bed was round. It had lots of big, fluffy pillows piled up against the headboard. It looked like Veronica's bed in an *Archie* comic she'd once seen.

Pepper checked over her shoulder. There was no one in sight, so she slipped quietly into the room and looked around. There were posters of teen idols on the wall. There was a vanity with makeup on a mirrored tray. There was a princess phone, and a record player too. Record sleeves were scattered on the carpet around it. There was a pile of discarded clothing on a chair in the corner. And sitting on the top of the pile was a hot pink miniskirt.

Pepper couldn't pull her eyes away from the skirt. Some of the girls at Pepper's school—mostly the older girls— had started wearing skirts like that. Pepper had thought of asking her mom if she could get one, but she had a pretty good idea what her mom would say. "Too much money for too little fabric," or, more likely, "You already have nice skirts. What about that navy-blue one I sewed for you last Christmas? It's lovely on you." The navy-blue skirt looked like a school uniform, and it went all the way down to her knees.

Pepper picked up the pink miniskirt, held it against her waist, and looked in the full-length mirror. The skirt was a little bit too wide, but even so, Pepper decided she definitely liked it. She turned this way and that, admiring her reflection.

At that moment someone else's reflection appeared in the mirror. Mrs. Ferguson was standing in the doorway behind her.

Pepper dropped the skirt and spun around. "Oh, I was just ... just ... trying to find the bathroom." She was too ashamed to look Mrs. Ferguson directly in the eye. There was an uncomfortable moment of silence as Pepper stared at the offending skirt that lay on the floor between them. "Sorry," she muttered, as an afterthought.

Mrs. Ferguson smiled. "The bathroom is the next room down the hall. This is April's room, my daughter's. She's out by the pool. Why don't you and Everett go out and meet her? You can have a swim if you'd like."

"Okay. Thank you." Pepper stepped awkwardly over the skirt as she left the room.

Pepper wasn't wearing her bathing suit under her clothes as she often did. That morning she'd checked the clothesline where she'd hung it overnight, but it had still felt damp. She hated putting on a wet bathing suit, but now she wished she had. Even so, she was eager to meet April. She and Everett found the teenage girl sunbathing on a chaise longue by the pool, listening to rock 'n' roll on a transistor radio. April was wearing a tangerine-coloured bikini and sunglasses. Her skin was bronzed to a perfect golden colour. Her hair, thick and straight and blonde, flowed halfway down her back.

"Hi," said Pepper. "I'm Pepper. This is my brother, Everett."

Everett hung back, completely silent.

April looked over the top of her sunglasses. Her gaze travelled from Pepper to Everett and back again. "Hi, there," she said. Her smile revealed a row of even white teeth.

"We're here with our grandma. She knows your mom and dad. Your mom told us to come out here and meet you," Pepper said.

April took off her sunglasses and looked towards the house, where they could see Grandma and Mr. and Mrs. Ferguson through the sliding glass doors.

"That's your grandma? Doesn't she live out on Shack Island?"

Pepper cringed. "Only in the summer," she said. "The rest of the year she lives in town. She has a toilet in town." Pepper snapped her mouth shut. Oh, why was she talking about toilets? What a stupid thing to say. Now April would think she was poor *and* peculiar.

But April didn't comment. She put her sunglasses back on and began to rub some suntan lotion on her legs.

Pepper shot Everett a glance. She tipped her head towards April and raised her eyebrows. Talk to her, she tried to communicate. Say something. Everett shook his head mutely.

Pepper sighed. Everett was hopeless when it came to girls. She turned back to April. "Your mom said we could swim in the pool, but we didn't bring our bathing suits."

"Maybe next time," said April. "Why don't you put your feet in at least?"

Pepper sat at the edge of the pool and dipped her feet in. The water was cool and refreshing. She wished she could race Everett across the pool the way she used to back at the community pool in Edmonton. She swung her legs and looked back over her shoulder. Everett had retreated to the shade under a tree, a good distance away from where April lay in the sun. Even if she jumped in with all her clothes on, she was certain she'd never get Everett to do it too.

What would it be like to be April? Pepper wondered. She was so lucky. She had a perfect family. A perfect life. She lived in a big house with a pool. She got to fly on planes to California. She had a round bed just like Veronica's. And she was beautiful.

Why couldn't Pepper's family be more like the Fergusons? Then Pepper had a crazy thought. It was so crazy she was almost afraid to think about it head-on, as if approaching the idea too directly would make it disappear. Her mind circled around and came back to it. What if— and her breath caught in her throat—what if the Fergusons *were* her real family?

Stop it, Pepper told herself firmly. The idea was nothing but wishful thinking. It couldn't be true. But … what if it was? Pepper recalled the note she had seen on Grandma's list, "Tell Pepper about the Fergusons," and the fleeting, secretive expression that had crossed Grandma's face.

Pepper felt dizzy. It was too silly to even think about. She pushed the idea to the back of her mind and tried to think about something else instead. Something useful. Practical. Like reading people's minds. She started to go through the seven steps she'd committed to memory from her ESP book. She relaxed her body. She tried to make her mind go blank. She continued to focus on April, waiting for something to pop into her mind.

But nothing happened.

Mrs. Ferguson appeared, chatting with Grandma at the door. Grandma waved. She pointed to her watch. Time to go, she mouthed.

Later that afternoon, after she'd helped Grandma with the pie, Pepper stepped out of the Periwinkle and noticed Everett standing on the beach. He was scanning the shoreline across the water with a pair of binoculars, unaware that Barry Brewster was walking towards him.

Barry tapped Everett on the shoulder. "Hey. What are you looking at?"

Everett lowered the binoculars with a start, too flustered to reply.

Barry laughed. "I bet you're watching April Ferguson over there on the point. I heard you were at her house today."

News travelled fast on Shack Island, Pepper thought.

Everett finally found his voice. "No. I was looking at the birds. Seagulls, I mean. I'm studying their habits." He took a notebook and pencil from his pocket. "I'm making some field notes."

Barry laughed again. "You don't fool me. You've got a crush on April Ferguson. Did you talk to her?"

"Sort of. A bit."

"Did you tell her about your *field notes*?"

Everett didn't reply.

Barry grabbed the binoculars and trained them on the point of land across the water. "Yeah. Just as I thought. There she is now, by the pool. Well, I can tell you this. You're wasting your time. She'll never go for a guy like you. Not in a million years."

Pepper considered Barry's claim. Suddenly it all made sense. Maybe Everett *did* have a crush on April. That would explain his odd behaviour when they'd met her at the pool. Sure, Everett was always shy with new people, but with April it had been a hundred times worse. Pepper looked at him now, sitting miserably on the beach, his glasses slipping down his nose. The bumps of his spine formed a skinny column visible even through his T-shirt.

She walked up to Barry. "Hey! Stop bugging my brother."

Barry looked her up and down. "Who are you?"

"My name's Pepper."

Barry turned to Everett. "Do you always make your kid sister stick up for you?"

Pepper grabbed the binoculars back from Barry. "Come on, Everett. Let's go."

That night Pepper had another strange dream. This one started with a crash and a flash of colour like a kaleidoscope shattering in a spray of splintered glass. The sound, jarring and brittle, echoed in the silence that followed. The flash was followed immediately by pitch black. Pepper couldn't see. She seemed to be standing on uneven ground. She reached up with both hands. Grabbed some sort of ledge in the dark. Then, suddenly, a terrible, sharp, searing pain. Something razor sharp sliced her hand to the bone.

Pepper jolted awake. She was covered in sweat and gasping for breath. Her hand was stinging. Was that a remnant of her dream? She held her hand up to the moonlight from the window. The skin was intact, but when she touched it, it felt as hot and swollen and prickly as if she'd been stung by a bee.

She lay down again, still breathing fast, staring into the night.

CHAPTER 6

The Sound of a Ghost

The next day, Grandma looked through the cooler on the porch and scratched her head.

"Isn't that the oddest thing? I was sure we had more food in here the last time I looked. Maybe I'm being absent-minded, but I thought we had some baloney left. Did someone eat it?"

"Not me," said Everett.

"Not me," said Pepper.

"Well, it couldn't have disappeared by itself. And ..." Grandma stood up and put her hands on her hips. "The Cheez Whiz is gone too."

"Maybe an animal got into the cooler in the night. A raccoon or something," Pepper suggested.

"I don't think so. The cooler is latched. It would be too tricky for any kind of animal." Grandma shook her head. "All I can say is it's a good thing we're going into town today. We'll have to stock up." She pulled a piece of paper from her pocket and added baloney and Cheez Whiz to her list.

Grandma planned her trip into town to get groceries, do laundry, fill the water bottles, collect her mail, and tend her garden. Pepper and Everett wanted to go so they could watch TV. Back home, they had a colour TV. Grandma still had a black-and-white one. Even so, it was better than no TV at all. Everett liked watching Westerns like *Bonanza* or variety shows like *The Smothers Brothers*. Pepper liked funny shows. *Get Smart*, about a bumbling secret agent, was one of her favourites. She also liked *Lost in Space*, a science fiction show about a family, stranded on a spaceship adrift in the universe, who had incredible adventures. Now that was an exciting family!

Grandma checked her mail when they arrived, but there was no letter from Pepper's mom and dad. She picked up the phone to call them while Pepper and Everett hovered nearby, then put the receiver straight back down again. "Party line," she said. "Sounds like Mrs. Williams from down the road is on right now. She talks a lot. We'll try again later."

Grandma made Pepper and Everett each weed a row in her garden. They raced through the job, both hoping to get to the TV first.

"I don't know why you two want to be inside on such a fine day," Grandma called out behind them as they rushed up the back stairs. "Shoes off in the house."

They kicked off their shoes, ran into the living room, and switched on the TV. Grandma came to the back door a little later and called, "Pepper. Everett. Don't forget to have a bath and wash your hair."

Pepper had her bath first and towelled off her hair with

one of Grandma's thin, stiff towels. Then Everett went into the bathroom and Pepper had the TV to herself. It was five o'clock, so the early movie was just starting. The opening music was low and threatening, with a tremulous sustained note laid on top. When the title came on the screen, *Invaders from Mars*, Pepper threw herself down on her stomach and propped herself up on her elbows.

The story was about a boy who wakes up one night during a thunderstorm. He sees a flying saucer land behind his house in a big sandpit area and then disappear. In the morning the boy tells his dad about the flying saucer. The dad goes to investigate, but when he returns he has a glassy-eyed stare and is acting like a robot. The boy notices a puncture mark along the hairline at the back of his dad's neck.

"Whatcha watching?" Everett said as he came back into the living room.

"*Invaders from Mars*. Shh ... It's coming to the good part."

Everett sat down. "I think I've seen it before. Is this the one about a UFO? Where space aliens take over all the people in town and turn them into zombies?"

Pepper glared at Everett, put her finger to her lips, and turned back to the television.

The boy in the movie looked through his telescope and saw the girl next door walk into the sandpit and then suddenly disappear underground.

"Pepper. Everett. Time to go," called Grandma from the back door.

"Just five more minutes."

The movie cut for a commercial break, then resumed. The boy was standing at the edge of the sandpit, looking for the neighbour girl, when he was sucked underground too. He was captured by two tall alien creatures with elongated heads and slit eyes. Pepper writhed around on the carpet, too excited to stay still.

"That was five minutes." Grandma came into the living room and switched off the TV.

Pepper and Everett groaned as they dragged themselves to their feet.

"Do you remember how it ends?" asked Pepper.

Everett shook his head. "Last time I just saw the first part. I've never seen the end."

"Well, what do you think happens?"

"I guess the kid gets turned into a zombie too."

"No, no! He has to escape and save the town."

"What difference does it make? It's just a movie."

"Oh! I almost forgot," Grandma interrupted. "We better try your mom and dad again." She picked up the telephone receiver, listened for a dial tone, and then dialed the number. "Remember, it's long distance. We'll have to keep it short," she said as the phone rang and rang at the other end. Finally she hung up. "That's a shame. I guess they're not home."

Pepper felt frustrated as she sat in the front of the Rambler on the drive back to Shack Island. Not only had they left before the end of the movie, she hadn't had a chance to talk to her mom and dad. She was surprised at how much she missed them. It was going to be a while before Grandma went into town again. Not that her parents probably even cared, she reminded herself. They likely hadn't given one thought to her the whole time she'd been gone. All they cared about was the baby.

She turned towards Everett in the back seat. "Wouldn't

it be neat if one day people could talk to each other whenever they wanted, no matter where they were?"

"You mean *mental telepathy*, like in that book you're reading?"

Pepper bristled at his scornful tone. "No," she said, although that was exactly what she'd meant.

Everett thought for a moment. "The way technology is developing now, I wouldn't be surprised if one day they'll invent a phone that you can carry around with you. It wouldn't have to be connected to the wall."

"How would it work though, if it wasn't connected?" wondered Pepper.

"Satellites."

"Satellites! What does that have to do with phones?"

"We're on the verge of amazing changes most people can't even fathom," Everett continued. "Computers, for instance. I think in the future they'll figure out how to make computers connect to each other. Then we'll all have our own personal computer and we can write back and forth to each other any time we want. We'll always know what's going on right at that very moment. We won't have to wait for the mail."

"What? Computers are huge! They take up a whole room. Not everyone is going to have space for a computer in their house."

"You don't understand, Pepper. They're figuring out how to make them smaller. One day everyone will have one."

"Yeah! Like that would ever happen!" Pepper stifled a snort. What a ridiculous idea. Then she had an idea of her own. "How about this? Maybe someone could invent a special tape recorder that would be able to tape a message if you phoned someone and they weren't home. Wouldn't that be great?"

"Someone's already invented that."

"Well, they should sell it! Everyone could have one on their phones. Things would be so much easier that way. If someone wasn't home, you could leave a message for them. And they could leave a message for you. Even if you lived far apart. Even if you could only get to your phone once in a while." Pepper's throat tightened up, and her eyes started to sting. She swallowed, blinked hard, and changed the subject. "You know something, Everett? You should seriously consider becoming an inventor. You'd be famous. You'd make a lot of money. How about this. You know that robot on *Lost in Space*? You could make a robot like that. You have practically all summer. That should be plenty of time. You could make the robot so it could time travel too."

Everett studied her for a moment, as if she was some sort of rare life form, then shook his head. "Sometimes I don't even know why I bother talking to you, Pepper."

The brush-off left Pepper feeling wounded. He wasn't the only one with brains, she wanted to say, but instead she clamped her mouth shut and pretended to be interested in the scenery passing outside the window.

That night Pepper stood outside the Periwinkle looking up at the vast velvety sky. The stars glittered like thousands of pieces of broken glass. Could there be a flying saucer, some sort of UFO, up there somewhere? And if there was, what if it landed nearby and turned everyone into space zombies? It was possible, Pepper decided. Very possible. In fact, tonight was exactly the kind of night it could happen. Pepper felt goosebumps rise on her skin. She wasn't going to stay outside a moment longer.

Just as she was turning to go back inside, she thought

she saw a flash of light over at Ghost Island. But when she looked again, it was gone.

When Pepper woke up the next morning, the first thing she thought of was the Fergusons. Her mind had been churning all night while she slept, and now one fully formed thought had crystallized. She wanted, more than anything, to belong to that family.

Pepper reviewed the facts. She had been adopted in Nanaimo, she knew that much. The Ferguson family was from Nanaimo as well. Mr. and Mrs. Ferguson were about the right age to be her real parents. There was the colour of Mrs. Ferguson's hair, too—strawberry blonde. It definitely had a touch of red in it. Pepper pulled on a strand of her own curly hair as she considered this. Maybe the idea wasn't so far-fetched.

And then there was that item on Grandma's list: "Tell Pepper about the Fergusons." Her heart started to race at the thought.

All through breakfast Pepper tried to work out some pretense to go back to the Fergusons' house. Once there, she hoped she might stumble on something to support her theory. She wasn't exactly sure what it might be. But surely, if she had been born into that family, something would eventually come to light. Some clue. Some slip of the tongue, perhaps. And then she thought of a scheme.

She unfastened her watch without Grandma and Everett noticing and put it in her pocket. "I think I left my watch at the Fergusons'," she said.

Everett looked at her, puzzled. "Weren't you wearing it yesterday?"

"No. I haven't been able to find it for a few days. I think

it's been gone since we went to the Fergusons'. I must have taken it off when I was in their house, or maybe when we were out at the pool. Do you think we can go over there today at low tide and look for it?"

"You go ahead. I don't think I'll go, though," said Grandma. "I'm planning on starting a new painting. I'm going to cart my things down the beach a ways. There's a spot I have in mind. I've got an idea for a piece with rocks and tidal pools and the light reflecting off the water like glass. But why not take Everett with you? That way at least one of you can keep an eye on the time and you won't get caught by the tide."

"Sure," said Everett so eagerly both Grandma and Pepper looked at him in surprise.

Grandma checked the tide book. "Low tide's about three today. Remember, you want to be back here no later than four, just to be on the safe side."

"Don't worry," they assured her.

When the tide was out far enough, Pepper and Everett set off. As they walked up the sun-dappled driveway to the Fergusons' house, they could hear Beatles music. Pepper knocked, but no one came to the door. The music continued to blare.

"Use the knocker," said Everett.

Pepper grabbed the big brass knocker and rapped loudly. The music stopped abruptly. They heard footsteps. Then the door opened. It was April.

"Oh, hi," she said, flashing her dazzling smile. "It's Pepper, isn't it? And Emmet?"

Pepper glanced at Everett. His pale skin had turned a startling shade of crimson. He opened his mouth and closed it again, without saying a word.

Pepper turned back to April. "Everett. His name is Everett. Sorry to bother you, but I think I left my watch here the other day. Have you seen it?"

April shook her head. "No. Maybe my mom or dad did. They're not here right now. You can come in and have a look around if you want."

"Thanks."

Pepper made herself busy looking around the living room where they had been sitting, checking between the couch cushions, looking under the magazines on the coffee table. She knew very well she wouldn't find the watch. It was safely hidden away in her shorts pocket.

Everett stood in the doorway, looking even geekier than usual, scratching the back of his head. It was nothing short of embarrassing having him hanging around all the time.

"Everett, why don't you go look out by the pool?" Pepper suggested.

As he went off, April watched him through the sliding glass doors, and then she turned to Pepper. "Your brother's never said anything to me. Not one word. Doesn't he like me?"

"What? No! He's shy around girls, that's all." But Pepper didn't want to talk about Everett. She turned in a slow circle, admiring the spectacular pool situated perfectly on the point of land, and the living room with its massive stone fireplace. "You're so lucky to live in a house like this. And go on trips to California. And everything."

"It's not all it's cracked up to be."

Pepper almost snorted. Not all it's cracked up to be? If she had everything April had, she'd never, ever take it for granted. Not for one minute. She cast another appreciative look around the room. And that's when she noticed the photo album on the bookshelf.

"Do you mind if I look at this?" she asked. "I just love looking at old photos."

April shrugged. "Sure. If you want."

Pepper slid the album out and flipped through the pages. There were snapshots of Mr. and Mrs. Ferguson when they were younger. On holiday. Standing by the house while it was still under construction. One of them looking down at a blonde baby—it must be April—swaddled in a blanket. A very young April smiling in front of a Christmas tree. April on a tricycle. Pepper kept flipping the pages, but there were no pictures of another baby.

She closed the album. "You're an only child? No brothers or sisters?"

"No. Just me."

"Didn't your mom ever want another baby?"

April looked surprised by the question. "Well, actually she did want another baby, but after she had me the doctor told her she couldn't have any more children."

Pepper groaned audibly, feeling suddenly deflated.

"Don't feel bad," April said. "My mom was disappointed for a while, of course, when the doctor told her. But that was a long time ago. It doesn't bother her anymore."

"They told my mom the same thing, but now she's having another baby."

"I guess that happens sometimes. But not for my mom." April paused. "You seem awfully interested in my family."

"Yeah. I guess I was kind of hoping ... Never mind."

Just then Everett came back in.

"Did you find the watch?" asked April.

Everett shook his head. A long silence followed.

April tried another question. "Do you like music?"

Everett nodded.

"What kind?"

"The Beatles."

While they were talking, Pepper furtively slid her hand into her pocket and placed the watch on the next shelf of the bookshelf. "Look!" she exclaimed. "Here it is! My watch!"

That night Grandma suggested they build a campfire on the beach. Pepper sat by the fire, poking the burning embers with a stick. Chloe was there and Everett and Grandma, all chatting away. Pepper didn't say much. She gazed off into the shadows, deep in thought. She still felt disappointed that the Fergusons weren't her real family. Oh, how she wished it could be so! If she was part of their family, her life would be perfect.

Then, through the gathering darkness, she saw a small flash of light on Ghost Island. It was the second time in as many days she'd seen a flash of light there.

"Is someone staying over on Ghost Island now?" she asked.

"No. It's still boarded up. They'll come out later in the summer, I expect," said Grandma.

Pepper thought again of the space alien movie. Was it possible that something from space had landed there? No, no, she told herself. It couldn't be. But the more she thought about it, the more she was convinced it was possible.

Chloe stood up. "I better head home before it gets any darker. 'Night, everyone."

Grandma stood up next. "I'm going in as well. It's cooling off. Are you two coming?"

"Uh-huh," Everett said.

Pepper's first instinct was to go inside with Grandma and Everett. After all, when it came to space aliens, being inside with other people had to be a whole lot safer than being outside by herself. But if she *did* go inside, and if there *was* something going on over at Ghost Island, she'd end up missing it. No, she decided, she was going to make herself stay outside and keep watch. "Not just yet," she told them.

Everett dumped a pail of water on the fire, apparently not trusting Pepper to do it, and followed Grandma up the beach towards their shack.

"Don't stay out too long," Grandma called over her shoulder.

Pepper kept a watchful eye out towards Ghost Island, even after it was so dark she couldn't see the shape of it. But there were no more sparks of light. The island remained blanketed in blackness. Then she heard a faint sound coming from the direction of Ghost Island. It was melodic, rising and falling like a voice. Or music. The eerie sound seemed to come and go, depending on the direction the breeze was blowing. Suddenly, Pepper remembered the ghost story Chloe had told her. The ghost of Ghost Island! It had to be. Shivers ran up and down Pepper's spine. She didn't wait a moment longer. She ran up the beach in the dark, tripping over driftwood and slipping in the sand. Then her feet were pounding up the stairs to the shack. She wrenched the door open and slammed it firmly behind her.

The following afternoon, as soon as the tide had retreated, Pepper picked her way across the narrow stretch of wet pebbly beach to Ghost Island. She approached the island cautiously, recalling the strange sound she'd heard. Then she remembered the last time she'd been there, and the dream-like image of the girl sitting on a ragged quilt. Could that have been some sort of ghost as well?

Pepper looked up the bank towards the shack. The windows were covered with plywood. The place, at first glance, seemed deserted. She noticed a cigarette butt on the bottom step of the stairs leading up from the beach. Strewn in the gravel below, more cigarette butts and burnt-out matches. Pepper warily climbed the stairs. There was a deck at the top that jutted out from the shack like a dilapidated stage. She crossed the weathered boards and checked the door. It was locked. Behind the building she found garbage tossed in the bushes: an empty milk carton, a bread bag, and some candy wrappers.

She turned back to the shack. And that's when her heart skipped a beat. One of the back window coverings had been pried off. The glass was smashed. She tiptoed closer and peered into the gloomy interior.

"Hello?" she called. Her voice echoed inside. It was a spooky sound.

Pepper took a few deep breaths, gathering her courage. She made sure there was no glass remaining on the window-sill, then hoisted herself up in one fluid motion. She got one knee planted on the sill. Then a cold breeze brushed the back of her neck like a ghostly hand against her skin. She almost lost her balance as she looked quickly over her shoulder. But there was no one there. She struggled to bring the other leg up and over, then hopped down to the floor inside.

"Hello," she called again.

It was deadly quiet. The room was dark and shadowy.

There was a stale, smoky smell about the place. The skin on the back of Pepper's neck tingled again. She had a strong impulse to climb back out the window. But she made herself stay put. Her eyes slowly grew accustomed to the gloom. She could make out a wood stove and a rocking chair. On the far side of the room stood a table covered by a checked, plastic-coated tablecloth. An object sat on the table. She tiptoed closer. It was a saucer full of stubbed-out cigarettes.

Then, through the partially open door to the next room, Pepper saw the corner of a bed, a bare mattress, a rumpled blanket … and a foot.

She gasped and drew back with a start. The ghost! Or possibly a space alien. Whatever it was, she'd seen it. She was shaking so hard she had to hold on to the table to steady herself. Maybe it was just a shadow. Maybe she'd imagined it. Pepper forced herself to inch forward again. And there it was. The foot. Pepper stared at it, but it didn't move. Ever so slowly, she edged closer and peeked around the door. The foot was connected to a leg, and the leg was connected to a young man. He was asleep. The blanket was askew, so she could see he was wearing only jeans. His chest was bare, and he was breathing slowly and deeply. His arms were well muscled. There was a dirty bandage on one of his hands and a stubble of reddish hair on his head, as if it had just been shorn.

And at that exact moment he opened his eyes.

CHAPTER 7

Hideaway

The young man in the bed sat straight up.

Pepper screamed.

"Who are you?" he shouted.

Pepper turned and ran for the window, but a split second later the young man leapt from the bed and caught her roughly by the arm. He smelled of smoke and sweat.

"Who are you? What are you doing here?"

"Please, let me go," Pepper cried out. His grip on her arm was so tight it made tears come to her eyes. "I didn't know you were here. I thought you were a ghost."

"A ghost?" He glared at her as he slowly released his hold. "Sit down," he ordered. He grabbed a chair and plunked it in the middle of the kitchen.

Pepper sat down.

"Now tell me. Why are you snooping around for a ghost?"

"I saw the cigarette butts, and I thought …"

"You were looking for a ghost who smokes cigarettes?"

Pepper gulped. "Either that or a space alien." It all sounded so stupid now.

The young man seemed startled by her answer, and a smile tugged his lips. Then he quickly became stern again. "You shouldn't be poking around strange places all by yourself. Hasn't anyone ever told you that?"

Pepper rubbed her arm. It still smarted. "I made a mistake. I'm sorry. Please, can I go now?"

"No." He shook his head firmly. "You sit right there. Don't move a muscle. I'm going to put a shirt on."

Pepper's heart was still racing. She looked towards the window. Maybe there was time to scramble out. But a moment later he came back pulling a T-shirt over his head. He studied her before he spoke. "Look. I'm sorry I was a little rough on you. You caught me off guard. Let's start again. What's your name?"

"Pepper."

"Pepper?"

"Yes. It's a nickname, but that's what everyone calls me."

"How come?"

"Because of my red hair. You know ... like a red pepper."

"Yeah. People call me Red sometimes. Even people who don't know me."

Pepper looked at the bristles that covered his scalp. His hair was about the same colour as hers. Something stirred in her mind, almost coming to the surface, but not quite. "What's *your* name?"

"Ray." He hesitated and looked her directly in the eye. "Listen. I'm going to ask you something, and it's important. You gotta promise me you won't tell anyone you saw me here. Okay? I don't want anyone to know."

"I won't," Pepper answered automatically. She didn't want to anger him again. But there was something else, something softer in his expression that made her want to trust him. She looked at the bandage wrapped around Ray's left hand. It was made from rags. "What happened to your hand?" she asked.

"Nothing. Just an accident."

"What kind of accident?"

Even before he spoke she knew what he was going to say.

"There was some broken glass on the windowsill. I didn't see it."

Just like in her dream! Pepper's eyes shot from his hands to his face, then to his bristly hair. Stubble! The other dream she'd had on the bus came rushing back to her—looking through a chain-link fence, the smell of evergreens, and the prickly feel of stubble on her shaved head.

Goosebumps ran up and down her back. Pepper tried to think clearly. There'd been her other dream too, the one about running down a road at night.

She couldn't help herself. She had to know. "Are you on the run from something?" Her voice was so quiet it was almost a whisper.

Ray's mouth tightened, but he didn't answer.

"Tell me. You are, aren't you?"

"Let's just say I'm lying low for a while." He took a deep breath. "I can see you're scared, but there's nothing to be afraid of. I won't hurt you. I won't bother anyone else, either. You can forget I'm even here. I was only planning on staying a short time. Until I figure out where to go next."

Pepper tried to make her voice sound calm. "Don't you have your own home to go to?"

Ray shrugged. "Not really. No home. No real family."

Pepper stared at him for a minute and then stood up shakily. "I'm going now. And you better not try to stop me!"

She went straight to the window and started to climb out.

"Here," Ray said, opening the door. "This way is easier."

Pepper ran down the beach without noticing where she was going. Crazy thoughts swirled in her head. Who was this guy? Why had she dreamed those dreams? And how was it possible her dreams had happened to someone she'd never met before? It was as if they had lived through the same experiences. As if they were one and the same.

As Pepper got closer to the Periwinkle, she saw Grandma sitting on the porch next to a woman with long, wavy hair and a cornflower tucked behind one ear. The woman wore a gauzy cotton blouse and had flowers embroidered in bright thread on her jeans.

"This is Starshine," said Grandma as Pepper came up the stairs. "She's living with her boyfriend, Huckle, over on Middle Island. Starshine, this is my granddaughter, Pepper."

"Peace," said Starshine. She held two fingers up in a *V*.

"Hi." Pepper sat down, realizing that this woman must be one of the hippies Chloe's mom had warned them about. Grandma didn't seem to mind her at all, though. In fact, she seemed to be enjoying Starshine's company.

"I'm teaching Starshine how to knit," said Grandma.

Pepper watched for a few minutes as Grandma demonstrated how to pick up a dropped stitch. It felt safe sitting quietly here with her grandma and Starshine, and her thoughts slowly calmed down. Then her curiosity got the better of her. "What are you doing here for the summer, Starshine?" she asked.

"We moved up here from the States. Huckle didn't want to take the chance of being drafted, so we decided to pack up our Volkswagen van and move to Canada."

"What do you mean, drafted?"

"You know the war in Vietnam? The United States is sending thousands of young men into the army to fight. The government wants even more soldiers, so they're going to have a lottery. All the days of the year are going to be put into a big barrel, with the dates drawn out in random order. If you're a man nineteen or older, and you have a birthday on the date that's drawn, you're going to war—whether you like it or not. It's the law. They'll keep going like that until they have enough soldiers. But Huckle and I don't agree with that. We don't want to be part of a big war machine."

"So is Huckle a draft dodger?" asked Pepper.

"Some people might call him that," said Starshine. "We like the name draft resister, though. We don't think the American government should make us fight in a war. Huckle made a choice not to fight. Lots of other people feel the same way. We participated in some big protest rallies. We did sit-ins. But the government won't listen. That's why we wanted to move up here to Canada. We got grilled at the border, but they let us in."

"What would happen if Huckle was drafted and he didn't go?" asked Pepper.

"They'd make him go to jail instead."

Pepper considered this for a moment. "You ran away because Huckle didn't want to go to war. He didn't want to kill anyone, right?"

"That's right. We believe in peace, not war. Flower Power and all that."

That evening, as the sun was sinking low and casting long shadows, Pepper sat on the front steps with Grandma. Grandma was reading one of the newspapers she'd brought back from town. Pepper was thinking about Ray. She'd promised to keep his existence a secret, but it made her uneasy. Maybe she should tell Grandma.

Just then Grandma pointed to a story on the front page. "Look at this," she said. "*Brannen Lake Boy Makes Brazen Escape.*"

"What's a Brannen Lake boy?" Pepper asked.

"Brannen Lake is a jail for juvenile delinquents. It's not far from here. Maybe fifteen, twenty minutes by car." Grandma peered at the story and clicked her tongue. "It says he escaped one night and they're looking for him. Eighteen years old with red hair."

Red hair! Pepper felt her breath catch and her heart go cold.

Grandma didn't notice. "Dear, dear. Imagine a young man in trouble with the law so early in his life. He must have had a rough start." She shook her head, turned the page, and kept reading.

Pepper had become as still as a statue, like a spell had been cast over her. Most people would tell someone about Ray, she thought. Maybe even report him to the police. He was running from something, she knew that much. He'd broken into that shack. He was trespassing. Then she thought of something else. Maybe Ray was the reason the food from their cooler had gone missing.

Pepper wasn't sure what to think of Ray. She had never

met anyone like him before. But she had to find out how a perfect stranger could have transported himself directly into her dreams.

So she didn't tell her grandma about him. She didn't tell Everett. She didn't tell anyone.

The next afternoon, Pepper timed her departure carefully. Grandma was busy working on a canvas, and Everett was reading.

"Bye," Pepper called out.

"Bye," said Grandma, absent-mindedly waving a paintbrush.

Everett didn't look up from his magazine.

No one asked where she was going. Pepper had planned to say she was headed to Chloe's, even though she knew Chloe and her mom had gone into town and wouldn't be back for several days. She was glad she didn't have to lie. She ran down the stairs and set off for Ghost Island.

The tide had gone out far enough that she could cross over. *You shouldn't be going back*, she said to herself. Anyone in their right mind would stay clear of someone who'd escaped from Brannen Lake. Something made her keep on walking, though.

She knew Ray could be dangerous, but there was a little part of her that didn't want to believe it. Pepper's plan was to spy on him, study his actions when he didn't know anyone was watching. She wouldn't let Ray catch her. She was too smart for that.

Once she got close to the cabin, Pepper crouched behind a rocky outcropping. There was no sign from her vantage point that the solitary shack was occupied. She would have to get closer. Steeling her nerves, she tiptoed cautiously up the steps, across the deck, and around the back. She listened. For several minutes there was only silence. Had Ray already moved on to some other hiding place? Then she heard a bump from inside the shack. Cautiously, she peeked in through the broken window. At first it was too dark to see much of anything, but as her eyes adjusted she could make out Ray's shadowy figure. He was stuffing things into a duffel bag. He took a last look around the room, slung the duffel bag over his shoulder, and picked up a guitar case.

When he opened the door, Pepper surprised herself. Before she could think twice, she ran around to the deck and confronted him.

Ray looked startled and a little scared. His eyes were wide. "You! What are you doing here again? You practically gave me a heart attack."

"Sorry."

"You better go home right away. You shouldn't be snooping around here."

Pepper looked at his duffel bag. "You're leaving, aren't you?" she asked.

"Maybe I am. But that's my business."

"But why? Why are you going?"

"I don't have a choice. I can't stay here anymore. It only takes one person to blow my cover. Now that you know I'm here, it's too risky for me to stay."

Pepper paused. She couldn't help feeling a little sorry for him. "Don't go because of me. I won't tell anyone you're here."

Ray studied her. Then he put his duffel bag down. "How do I know I can trust you?"

"I swear I won't tell a soul." Pepper put her hand up in

the air as if she was taking an oath. "I won't breathe a word. Promise."

Ray still looked doubtful. "Did you bring anyone here with you?"

"No. Honest. It's just me."

Ray glanced around, and his shoulders relaxed. "Okay. But you better get going, and don't come back. It's safer that way."

"All right," Pepper agreed. "But since I'm here now, can I ask you a couple of questions?"

Ray's wariness returned. "What for?"

"Just a couple. Okay? Then I'll go away and you can forget all about me. It will be like we never met."

Ray sighed and put his guitar case down beside the duffel bag. He opened the shack's door wide enough so that sunlight slanted in and pooled on the worn linoleum tiles. He pulled two kitchen chairs into the light and they both sat down. "Go ahead. Shoot."

Ray was only a few inches taller than Everett, Pepper noted, but his shoulders were almost twice as wide. He looked strong. There was a smooth confidence about the way he moved. And you could tell from the slow, easy way he smiled that he knew he was good-looking.

"How old are you?" she asked.

"Eighteen."

Pepper took in a sharp breath. "Why are you hiding here?"

Ray shifted in his chair. "It's complicated ... sort of hard to explain."

"How do I know you're not some kind of murderer or something?"

"Look, Pepper. I haven't done anything wrong. Not really.

If I hadn't just met you maybe I'd tell you the whole story, but I'm not going to get into it now."

Pepper shook her head. "No," she said. "If you want me to keep this a secret, you'll have to be honest with me. Did you run away from Brannen Lake?"

"Brannen Lake? What are you talking about?"

"It was in the newspaper. Some guy escaped from Brannen Lake, a jail for juvenile delinquents."

"What does that have to do with me?"

"There was a description: eighteen years old, red hair."

"Oh, I see what you're thinking ..."

"Is it you?"

"No, it's not."

She studied him for several moments, her eyes narrowed.

Ray looked straight at Pepper, as if he had nothing to hide.

"Okay. I believe you," she said finally, though she wasn't actually sure she did. "I think I figured out why you're here, then."

"You have?"

"Well, not exactly. I'm taking a guess, but I think you're here because you didn't want to be drafted."

She could see Ray was surprised. "What makes you think that?"

"There're some people staying over on Middle Island. My grandma made friends with them. One of them is called Huckle and his girlfriend is Starshine. Starshine told me all about it. They left the States because they don't believe in war. They made it across the border into Canada. So I wondered if that's what you did too."

Ray nodded slowly. "You're a smart girl to figure that out."

"Why didn't you want to tell me? Maybe I would have done the same thing if I was in your position."

"Not everyone thinks that way, Pepper. Lots of people think it's a man's duty to fight for his country. They call draft dodgers cowardly. They call them traitors. Some people call them names a whole lot worse than that."

"My grandma doesn't mind them. Maybe you can meet her one day."

"Maybe." Ray sounded vague.

"How are you getting food and water while you're hiding?" Pepper asked.

"I've managed so far. I found toothpaste, soap, even a razor here. I've been drinking water from the rain barrel but it looks dirty, and there're bugs in it. I'd boil it but I don't want anyone to see the smoke from the wood stove. As far as food, there were some canned beans and crackers on the shelf, but I went through them pretty quick. Sometimes I have to go ... foraging."

Pepper thought of the baloney and Cheez Whiz that had gone missing from Grandma's cooler. Stealing food, breaking into cabins ... what else might Ray be capable of? But she pushed the thought from her mind.

"Maybe I could bring you something to eat," said Pepper. It would give her an excuse to come back again and find out more about him.

"It's not a good idea for you to be coming over here. Remember? We talked about that already."

"Don't worry. I'll be careful. No one will suspect anything," Pepper insisted as she got up to leave. Ray looked stern, but he didn't say a word.

That evening, while Grandma and Everett were outside,

Pepper took some slices of bread and a can of tomatoes from the shelf in the kitchen. They were items she hoped would not be missed. She filled a jar from the water jug and screwed the lid on tightly. She also took some bandages from Grandma's first-aid kit. She hid everything under her bed.

Later, as she lay in bed waiting to fall asleep, an unsettling idea formed in her mind. Ray had red hair. She had red hair. He'd said he was on his own, that he had no family. She'd lost her real family. And then there was the ESP connection she seemed to have with him through her dreams. She didn't have that with anyone else, no matter how hard she tried.

What if … what if Ray was her brother? But that was crazy. There were plenty of redheads in the world, and they weren't all related. And what were the chances she would just happen upon her own brother like this? Practically none, she told herself. He was American. She was Canadian. It was ridiculous. Preposterous. Of course he wasn't her brother. No, she decided, she would not think about it for one more second.

Still, the following day, when Pepper snuck over to Ghost Island to deliver the items to Ray, she couldn't resist asking him more questions. "You said you don't have a home or family," she started off.

"Yeah. That's right."

"What happened? How come you're on your own?"

Ray shrugged. "That's just the way it is."

"I don't either. Have a family. A real family, I mean."

"Why not?"

"I'm adopted. I don't know anything about my real

family, except that I was adopted in Nanaimo." Pepper leaned forward. She wanted to see his expression. "Were you adopted too?"

Ray looked surprised at first, and then something seemed to register. He looked straight back at her, his eyebrows raised slightly. A pause. "No."

Pepper thought maybe she hadn't heard him right. "You weren't?"

"No."

Pepper slumped back in her chair. Of course the whole idea had been nonsense. Too active an imagination, she told herself. That was her problem.

But in the next moment Ray added, "No one wanted to adopt me."

Pepper sat forward again. "What do you mean?"

"I was in foster care … because no one wanted to adopt me."

Pepper felt her muscles tense with excitement. The air felt electric. Was Ray about to say aloud what she was thinking?

But the moment passed. Ray reached for his guitar and strummed a few chords. "Do you want to hear something?" he asked, as if nothing had happened.

Pepper nodded. She felt dizzy, like she'd been twirling in circles.

"It's a bit awkward with this bandage," Ray said, "and it takes a while for my hand to limber up, so bear with me." He played a simple melody on the strings. The next verse was more complex. Soon he was strumming and picking so rapidly, his fingers were a blur. When he started to sing, his voice was low and resonant. There was an intensity to the song that seemed to come straight from his soul. The words told a story of a young man who didn't want to go to war, and Ray's face looked vulnerable as he sang.

Pepper was transfixed. She felt a surge of sympathy so strong it was almost overwhelming. Was it possible she was looking into the face of her own brother? Her eyes teared up, but she wiped her cheeks quickly, hoping he wouldn't notice.

After Ray had played the last note, Pepper clapped enthusiastically. "That was good! You should be performing on stage. Where'd you learn to play like that?"

"Here and there. I used to play more rock 'n' roll, but lately I like to play folk songs. Protest songs. That kind of thing. I write my own songs too."

"Was that one of them?"

"Uh-huh."

"Would you write a song for me?"

"I might just do that." He grinned as he put down the guitar. "One day."

Later, as she walked back to the main island, Pepper hummed a few bars from the song Ray played for her. She'd never heard anyone sing like that, just for her. She wished she could tell her new friend Chloe about it.

That night, Pepper tossed in her bed. She couldn't stop thinking about Ray. He was the kind of brother she'd always wanted. He was exciting. He was daring. And not only that, he played the guitar and wrote songs. All the doubts she'd had about him seemed to fade into the background. She'd hidden more food for him under her bed. She was planning to take it to him tomorrow, and there was something very important she had to talk to him about.

The next day, as soon as Pepper saw Ray, the words

tumbled out of her mouth. "I think we might be brother and sister."

Ray laughed. "What? Brother and sister? Where'd you get a silly idea like that?"

Pepper felt her face flush red. Still, she wouldn't be put off. "But what if we were?"

Ray's smile faded. "You can't be serious."

"I am."

Ray stared at her. Then he got up from his chair and walked around the room a couple of times, rubbing a hand over the stubble on his head. He sat down again and looked at Pepper. His usual confidence had been replaced with uncertainty.

He shook his head. "I don't know, Pepper. It doesn't seem very likely."

"Not impossible, though, right?" Pepper couldn't shake the idea. "I just want to find my real family. That's all." She stood up shakily. "Let's just think about it. Could I come again tomorrow?"

Ray hesitated, then nodded. "I'll be here."

CHAPTER 8
Flesh and Blood

Pepper woke up early the next morning. The tide was already low. She checked carefully up and down the beach. No one was in sight. She ran all the way over to Ghost Island, casting a few glances back over her shoulder to make sure she wasn't being seen. She bolted up the stairs of Ray's shack and knocked on the door.

Ray covered his mouth as he yawned and let her in. They sat in their usual spots at the kitchen table.

He regarded her solemnly. "I've got something to tell you," he said. "I did have a little sister. And she was adopted."

Pepper inhaled sharply. "I knew it!"

"Let's not get ahead of ourselves. When were you adopted?" Ray asked.

"Ten years ago."

"You said in Nanaimo, right?"

"Right."

"And Pepper's your nickname. What's your real name?"

"The name I was given when I was born is Allison. They didn't change it when I was adopted."

"Allison!" A satisfied look crossed Ray's face.

There was an arch in Ray's eyebrow that made Pepper pause for a moment. But then his expression changed and she forgot all about it.

"That was my little sister's name," Ray said. He laughed a shaky, short-lived laugh.

Pepper was so excited the room started to spin around her. She had to calm herself before she spoke. "There's something I don't get, though. You're American. I'm Canadian. How can we be brother and sister?"

"That's true. I *am* American. I was born there. But I grew up in Canada." He looked Pepper right in the eye, then added, "In fact, I grew up in Nanaimo."

Once again, Pepper felt a jolt of electricity pass between them. Pinpricks of tears stung her eyes.

"This is pretty weird, you know," Ray said. "I mean, one minute I'm minding my own business, and then suddenly you show up. What are the chances?" He thought for a moment. "What made you think we were related?"

"I just had a feeling." Pepper didn't want to say anything about her ESP dreams. "Mostly it was the red hair, I guess."

"Brother and sister," Ray mused, shaking his head. "Flesh and blood."

Pepper's thoughts were coming a mile a minute. "I never thought I'd have a brother who's on the run, though," she blurted before she could stop herself.

"Oh …" Ray sounded disappointed and a little ashamed. "Pepper, I made a couple of mistakes. I know that. It hasn't been easy for me. Not by a long shot. But I don't want to make excuses. I don't blame anyone but myself. And the truth is, I'm not proud of myself right now. But I'm going to turn my life around. I can be a good brother to you." He looked her right in the eye. "Will you give me a chance?"

Pepper gulped. A couple of mistakes, Ray had said. Was there something he wasn't telling her? It was all pretty confusing, but she felt her head nod up and down. She wanted to trust him, more than anything. And there was so much she needed to find out. "What happened to our mom and dad? Why did they give us up for adoption?" she asked.

"Dad left us before you were born. Mom used to say we were better off without him."

"Where'd he go?"

"Don't know. Don't care." He shrugged. "Mom used to say that too."

"But why did she give us up?"

"She got sick. She couldn't go to work. She spent most of the time on the couch. She'd give me some money, and I'd get groceries from the corner store. I tried to look after her. I tried to look after you, too. I kept hoping she'd get better. But she didn't. She had to go to the hospital. And then some social workers came and took us away. We were supposed to stay in a foster home until Mom was well again. So we went there, and we waited. We waited ... and ..." He stopped.

"And what?"

"You used to cry. The people in the foster home would pick you up and carry you around. They thought you were cute—so little, with your curly red hair. But they didn't think I was cute. They said I was a bad apple."

"How come?"

"One day I ran away. I was trying to get to the hospital.

I didn't even know where it was. Before I could get very far, they caught me and took me back."

Ray got up, took a cigarette from the pack on the kitchen table, sat down again, and lit it up. "This is my last one," he said. He took a long draw on it, then continued. "Mom was sick a long time. After a while, some more people came and took you away. I thought it was just for a short time. I didn't know I'd never see you again. I didn't know they were adopting you for good."

"Did anyone tell you where I went?"

He shook his head. "No. They've got rules about that."

"What happened to you?"

"I guess no one wanted to adopt me. One day they told me I had to go to another foster home. After a month or so, they sent me to another one. And then another one, and then another. It was like that. I was never in one place long enough to really get to know anyone, to feel like I belonged."

Pepper watched him take another drag on his cigarette and then blow a smoke ring. He was acting cool, but his voice sounded shaky.

"What happened to our mother?" she asked.

"Mom?" He glanced at Pepper and then looked away. "No one thought she was going to make it. Not even her. That's why she wanted us to be with good families who would look after us. But she surprised everyone. She *did* get better, after all."

"But didn't she want to take us back again?"

"Sure, she did. But by then, you'd already been adopted, and I was too much of a handful for her. She decided to move back to California. She'd only come up here in the first place because of our dad. California is warmer, lots of sun. She thought she'd get better faster down there. She wrote me a couple of letters and explained everything."

Pepper was shocked to hear their mom had left without them. What kind of mom would do that? At least her real mother was still alive, though, Pepper told herself. But California was such a long way away. "Have you heard from her lately?" she asked.

"Well … it's been a while. I've moved around so much. She's moved a few times too. We've sort of lost touch over the past few years."

"What's she like? Does she have red hair like us?"

"Well, sort of. Reddish. More of an auburn, I'd guess you'd call it."

"What's her name?"

"Beverly. Everyone called her Bev. On Sunday mornings she used to cook us pancakes. She'd read us stories before bedtime, and she'd talk in all the different characters' voices. She laughed a lot. She only had a couple of nice dresses, but when she got dressed up she looked pretty. She'd wear this perfume called French Lilac. She kept a big bottle of it on her dresser. Sometimes, even now, I think I can smell it. Just a whiff every once in a while."

As Ray described the perfume, Pepper thought she could remember the smell too. Sweet. Light. Lovely as a spring breeze.

"So," Ray said. "How about you?"

Pepper told him about her life with her adopted family, about Everett, about the new baby coming, about how she'd been sent away to Shack Island for the summer. "They switched my room for the baby's, and now I have to be up in the attic," she finished.

97

"Doesn't sound too bad. Could be a lot worse," Ray said. He stubbed out his cigarette in a saucer.

Pepper clamped her mouth tightly and crossed her arms. She could have explained it better, but what was the point? She'd only sound like a whiner. And it was true, compared to the life Ray had, her problems didn't seem so bad.

As Pepper trudged home before the tide came in again, she thought over everything she'd learned about her real family. There was a dad who wasn't even in the picture. A mom who had left two children behind. And a brother who'd bounced from one foster home to another. It certainly wasn't the perfect family she'd been hoping for. Her real family had turned out to be nothing at all like the Fergusons. And it was going to take some time to get used to the idea.

Early the following morning Chloe came to the door. "I'm back again," she announced. "Did you miss me? I went to the movies twice when I was in town. Do you want to do something with me today?"

The tide was on its way out, and Pepper knew that it wouldn't be long before she'd have to leave for Ghost Island. "What did you have in mind?"

"I don't know. What do you want to do?"

"How about we build a fort? I saw a good place up on the bluff."

Chloe made a face. "Nah. That's kid's stuff."

"Do you have a better idea?"

"Well, no."

"Okay, then. But I'll have to do it later. I've got some things I have to do first."

"Like what?"

"Um …" For a second her mind went blank. "Help my grandma," she mumbled.

"Oh. Okay. See you later. And don't take too long."

Pepper stuffed some items for Ray into a brown paper bag. As she was going down the steps her grandma called out behind her, "Did I hear you say something about helping me today?"

Pepper stopped. "Uh-huh."

"I've got some peas you can shell."

"Okay. I'll be right back," Pepper said and jumped down the rest of the stairs before her grandma could ask where she was going or what was in the bag.

She slipped quickly over to Ghost Island and knocked on the door, out of breath from running the whole way. As soon as Ray opened the door, she handed him the bag. "I can't stay. My grandma's waiting for me."

She thought Ray looked disappointed. As she turned to go, he said, "You know, sometimes you remind me of Mom."

"I do?"

"Yeah. You have the same personality: fun loving, lots of imagination, open to adventure. Even when Mom was sick, she still had that spark. You have it too. You're both a special kind of person."

Pepper kept turning the phrase over and over in her head as she walked back to the main island. She was a special kind of person, just like her mom.

That afternoon, as she and Chloe built the fort, Pepper found herself worrying about Ray. She couldn't keep taking him food. Grandma would get suspicious. Because of the tide, Ray could only walk off Ghost Island for a short time, once during the day and once at night, to try to find food for himself. She was pretty sure he didn't have a boat. And whenever he did leave the island, he'd have to be careful that no one saw him.

The two girls dragged logs from the beach to the top of the bluff and propped them up like a lean-to against the rock. It was hard work. They used branches to fill in the spaces between the logs. Finally Chloe climbed inside. "This fort is super cool," she said. "Come in and see."

Pepper grinned. "Didn't you say this morning you were too old for forts?"

"Well, maybe I was wrong about that. It was kind of fun making it. And I have to admit it turned out pretty good."

Pepper climbed in beside her. "We could have a picnic in here," she said.

"We can spy on people down on the beach."

"Yeah! No one can see us up here."

"Maybe we could camp out one night."

"How about tonight?" Pepper was excited by the thought.

"Ask your grandma if you can! I've got an extra sleeping bag. And I can bring marshmallows."

"Okay. I'll bring a flashlight."

Grandma and Chloe's mom both agreed, so right after supper they met back at the fort with all their supplies for the night. They watched the fishing boats off in the distance. The sound travelled so well across the water they could hear the fishermen talking to each other. Below them, in the bay, Grandma was teaching Everett to row. The little boat zigzagged slowly towards Middle Island and back. The sun sank lower and lower in the rose-coloured sky until there was nothing left of it. The evening air was cool. Darkness crept in around them. The breeze stirred the bushes, making them rustle.

Pepper sat cross-legged, her sleeping bag draped around her like a cape. "Do you believe in ESP?" she asked.

"I don't know."

"I do. Sometimes I think I can almost do it—read people's minds, I mean."

"Really?"

"Yeah. Do you want to try?"

"Okay," agreed Chloe.

"You think of a shape, okay? A circle, or a square, or a star. And I'll see if I can guess it. Are you ready?"

"Yup."

"Are you thinking of it?"

"Yup."

"Is it a circle?"

"No."

"Square?"

"No."

"Well, it's a star, then."

"No. It's a triangle."

"A triangle! A triangle wasn't one of the shapes. Circle, square, or star. Those are your choices."

"Sorry. I've never done this before. I didn't know there were rules."

"Let's try again. Okay … is it a square?"

"I wasn't ready."

Pepper sighed. "Tell me when you're ready, then."

"I'm ready. No, wait. What are my choices again?"

"Circle, square, or star."

"Okay. Now I'm ready."

Just then there was more rustling in the bushes nearby. This time it sounded loud, like some kind of animal.

"What's that?" said Chloe.

They listened, but the noise had stopped.

"Maybe it's a raccoon. Or an owl." Pepper pulled her sleeping bag closer. "Was it a circle?"

"Was what a circle?"

"The shape I'm supposed to be guessing! Pay attention."

"Oh. I forget."

"Chloe!"

"Sorry. I'm not good at this ESP stuff. Besides, it gives me the heebie-jeebies. And it doesn't help that there are all sorts of creepy noises out there."

The noise in the bushes started again.

"Do you think it's a bird rustling around in the leaves?" whispered Chloe.

"Maybe." Pepper was starting to feel uneasy as well. "It sounds pretty loud, though. It sounds loud enough to be a person."

"What would a person be doing out at this time of night?"

"I don't know."

The noise continued. It definitely sounded like someone walking through dry leaves. Pepper thought of murderers and kidnappers. Or maybe it was Ray out looking for food. She switched on the flashlight. Immediately the noises stopped. She shone the light across the trees, rocky out-croppings, and patches of thistles and grass. There was no one to be seen.

"Let's leave the light on," said Chloe.

"Okay, but just for a minute. I don't want to run the batteries down."

When she switched the flashlight off, the night seemed even blacker, pressing down around them. Pepper thought of Ray again. He'd have eaten the food she'd taken him in no time. The water would be gone by now too. He was going to starve. What kind of sister was she, letting her own brother starve?

"Chloe," said Pepper, "I'm going to tell you a secret. But you have to promise not to tell."

"Promise."

"Pinky swear?"

"Pinky swear."

They linked their baby fingers, and then Pepper said, "Okay. You know how I'm adopted? Well, I've found my brother. Only he didn't turn out to be the kind of brother I thought he would be …"

"Wait a minute!" said Chloe. "What do you mean, you found your brother? What about Everett?"

"I mean my real brother. I met this guy, and he has red hair like me, and he has a sister who was adopted. So I figured it out."

"Here? On Shack Island?"

"Yeah. That's what I'm saying."

Chloe sounded doubtful. "But how can you be sure he's your brother?"

"I just know he is." Pepper launched into the whole story about Ray being a draft dodger and hiding out on Ghost Island. "We have to get him some more food, or else he's going to starve to death," she finished up.

"You're going way too fast," said Chloe. "Let me get this straight. Your real brother's a draft dodger?"

"That's right. And we have to figure out how to get food for him, and—"

Chloe grabbed Pepper's arm. "A draft dodger?"

"Yes. A draft dodger. Is something wrong with your ears?"

"You know my mom doesn't like hippies or draft dodgers. She says they can't be trusted."

"They're not that bad, Chloe. You just have to give them a chance. Starshine told me her boyfriend, Huckle, is a draft dodger too. They're the hippies who are living over on Middle Island."

"You've been talking to the hippies on Middle Island?"

"Yes. My grandma has too. She's even teaching Starshine how to knit."

"If your grandma likes draft dodgers so much, how come she doesn't give your real brother some food? Or why don't those hippies on Middle Island do it? They could help him out."

"Ray made me promise not to tell anyone."

"Why?"

"I don't know. He just did. So, are you going to help me or not?"

"Pepper, this doesn't seem like a good idea."

"Please?"

"I'll think about it. Maybe."

"Maybe yes, or maybe no?"

"Just maybe." The noise in the bushes started up again, closer this time. "Listen," said Chloe. "There it is again." She stood up. "I'm gonna go home now."

"Me too," said Pepper.

They gathered up their belongings. "It wasn't like we were going to stay the *whole* night," said Chloe.

"Of course not."

The next morning, after Pepper's grandma had gone off to work on her latest painting, Chloe arrived at the door of the Periwinkle with two huge bags of groceries. "I'm just doing it this once. Okay? It's not because I want to do it. It's only because you're my friend. So don't ask me to do it again."

Everett was still sleeping, so Pepper replied in a whisper. "Thanks. You're a real pal, Chloe."

The girls found a spot on the beach to look through the bags. There was Velveeta cheese, Spam, canned tomatoes, two loaves of bread, blackberry jam, apples, Rice Krispies, and a carton of milk.

"Isn't your mom going to miss all this?" asked Pepper.

Chloe grinned. "Nope. I told her we needed it for provisions."

"Provisions? For what?"

"Our fort. What kind of fort would it be if we didn't have provisions?"

"Good thinking."

Chloe twisted the jam lid until it opened with a pop. She stuck in her finger and licked it off. "Mmm. This stuff is great. My mom makes it herself. Want some?"

Pepper shook her head and looked towards Ghost Island. The tide was low enough now to walk across. "It looks like the coast is clear. We better get going. We can each take a bag. Just try not to look too obvious in case anyone sees us."

Once they reached Ghost Island, though, Chloe hung back nervously. "Is Ray dangerous?" she said.

"Um ... probably not. At least, I don't think so," said Pepper.

"Well, I'm not going up there. I'm staying out of sight while you talk to him." Chloe sat down on the bottom step.

Pepper climbed the rickety steps to the deck and knocked on the door. "It's me, Pepper. I brought some food," she called.

Ray opened the door. "Wow! Two bags. Thanks a lot." He took them from her arms.

Pepper hesitated for a moment. "Ray?"

"What?"

"You know how you didn't want me to tell anyone you're here?"

"Yeah?" His eyes narrowed.

"I needed to get some more food for you, but I didn't want my grandma to notice, so I asked my friend to help."

Ray almost dropped the bags. "You what?"

"My friend, Chloe … I asked her to help. She got all this stuff from her place."

Ray's eyes blazed. "Great! That's just great. It was supposed to be a secret. That was the deal."

"I was trying to help."

"Pepper! For the love of …" He pressed his lips together, then took a deep breath. "It doesn't help if everyone knows I'm here."

"I didn't tell everyone. I only told Chloe."

He set the bags down. "She's not going to go and blab, is she?"

"No. She swore not to tell anyone. You can ask her yourself, if you want. She's sitting outside at the bottom of the steps."

Pepper went and coaxed Chloe to come up the stairs. Ray looked her up and down. Then he smiled his charming smile. "Chloe, right?"

She nodded.

"I'm Ray, Pepper's brother. It's a pleasure to meet you. Thank you for the groceries. That was nice of you. A decent thing to do." He caught Chloe's gaze and held it, still smiling. "You're not going to say anything about me being here, are you?"

"Oh, no. I won't breathe a word," said Chloe, smiling back. There was a piece of blackberry stuck on her front tooth.

Later, as the girls walked back to the main island, Chloe couldn't stop talking. "I think your brother's really cute. He looks like Davy Jones."

"Who's that?"

"The singer from the Monkees, of course. You know the band the Monkees, don't you? They're on TV."

Pepper had seen the show once or twice, but she wasn't too sure which one in the band was Davy Jones. None of them looked much like Ray to her.

Chloe didn't wait for Pepper to respond. "Davy Jones has long, brown hair, and he's on the short side, and he has an English accent, but other than that, he really reminds me of Ray. I wouldn't mind taking Ray some more food. There's a package of cookies I could take over next time. The kind with the creamy stuff in the middle. I think he'd like those. I could probably find some other stuff too. Did you see those big muscles on his arms? And the way he smiled at me?"

"Chloe!"

"What? All I'm saying is he's cute."

Pepper didn't reply.

"Very cute," Chloe said again, more to herself than anyone else.

Pepper ignored her. She'd liked it better when it had been just her and Ray. Now she had to share Ray's attention with Chloe. She picked up a small, flat rock and tried to skip it across the water. But instead of hopping along the surface, it sliced straight into the water and disappeared.

CHAPTER 9

The Straight Story

"Tell us how you got over the border into Canada," Pepper said.

She was sitting with Ray and Chloe on the deck of the Ghost Island shack. From where they sat they couldn't see any of the shacks on the other islands, and no one could see them.

"Oh, yes, Ray, tell us," Chloe said.

Pepper looked at her friend sharply, noticing for the first time something odd about her eyes. Eyeshadow. Chloe was wearing blue eyeshadow.

Ray shook his head. "You don't want to hear that story."

"Yes, we do!" said Chloe, smiling sweetly and leaning towards him.

Earlier that morning, Chloe had showed up at Pepper's door with another bag of food, eager to go back to Ghost Island. Now Pepper felt irritated that Chloe was trying to be the centre of attention.

Ray shrugged. "Well, it was pretty nerve-wracking. I wasn't sure if I'd make it into Canada. The officer at the border didn't blink, just stared at me. I told him I was coming up here for a visit. He asked me if I was in university. I said I wanted to go one day. He asked what kind of work I do. He looked at me like he could see right through me, right into my soul."

"Oh, Ray. I'd have been so nervous if that was me," said Chloe.

"Oh, I was nervous, believe me. I just tried not to show it. You can't imagine what a relief it was when he finally gave my papers back and said, 'Welcome to Canada. Have a good visit.' And that was it."

Ray picked up his guitar and started tuning it.

"You're so brave!" said Chloe. "I'd be too scared. Wouldn't you, Pepper? Wouldn't you be too scared?"

Pepper looked again at Chloe's startling blue-lidded eyes. Only a few days ago Chloe had said draft dodgers were cowards, and now she was acting like they were the bravest things going.

Pepper had a funny feeling something wasn't quite right about Ray's story. The way he'd told it, too quickly for them to ask any questions, made her uneasy. His eyes met hers briefly and then slid from her gaze. It made her think of the way a broken egg slips from the counter onto the floor.

"Can you play something for us?" asked Chloe.

Ray smiled obligingly, launching into a sad song about a city boy who yearned to live by the sea.

At the end of the song, Chloe fluttered her eyes. "Can you play another one?"

Pepper was enchanted by Ray's singing. She wished she could hear another song too, but suddenly she remembered the tide. She stood up quickly. "We'd better be getting home," she said. "Before it's too late."

On the way back, Chloe chattered about Ray. But Pepper wasn't listening. All she could think about was the wistful way Ray's song had made her feel.

Pepper went digging for clams with her grandma the following morning when the tide was out. She cast a furtive glance towards Ghost Island, but the shack appeared completely abandoned.

"Look for little holes in the sand," Grandma said. "That's how you can tell where to dig." She was wearing her baggy Bermuda shorts and was carrying a pail and a spade.

When a spray of water shot up from one of the holes, Pepper jumped back.

"That's a clam down there," Grandma said, and she stuck her spade into the sand. After a few moments of digging she pulled out a shell and dropped it in the pail. "We'll have clam chowder tonight. I've got potatoes and carrots for it. Look. Here's another one! If we get enough I'll make a big soup that will last us a couple of days. It's amazing how fast we've been going through food lately. It just seems to fly off the shelves."

Pepper kept her head down.

"I can't figure out where it's all going," Grandma continued. "We got so many bags of groceries last time we were in town."

"Everett's a big eater," said Pepper.

"He is? You'd never know it to look at him. He seems more of a picky eater to me. Sometimes he doesn't even finish his dinner."

"He likes to snack late at night," said Pepper. "That's

when he gets hungry. I hear him in the kitchen quite often."

"You do? I've never heard him."

"Oh, yes. Most nights. Probably you're already asleep." Pepper was pleased with her cleverness.

"Well, you'd never know it to look at him," Grandma said again. "But I suppose that would explain it."

As Pepper bent over, digging in the sand, she cast another glance towards Ghost Island. There were a few things about Ray's story that didn't make sense. First of all, he'd told her he was eighteen. But Starshine had said the draft was for older boys and men. And even if it were possible that Ray could be drafted, wouldn't he be safe now that he'd crossed the border? Huckle had done the same thing, and he and Starshine weren't hiding.

Pepper went over and over these things in her mind, but she couldn't make any sense of them.

Just then a clam squirted a shot of water up through a hole in the sand. It hit her right in the eye.

Later that day, Pepper picked her way along the beach to Chloe's. The rocks were slippery in places with slimy green seaweed. In other places barnacles crunched underfoot. Out in the bay she could see Everett practising rowing. He was able to go out on his own now, still slow, but not zigzagging as much as he used to. Pepper liked hopping log to log, checking to see what the tide brought in. She found a glass Japanese fishing float, delicate as a bubble. There was a splintered oar, and a snarl of yellow rope. Most of her finds were driftwood, all shapes and sizes. The thing she liked about beachcombing was the thought that each item had likely started miles and miles away, and the tides had brought it to this particular beach for her to discover. Chance, fate, and luck had all played a part.

She climbed the stairs to Chloe's shack. Chloe was on the veranda reading a *Tiger Beat* magazine. "Look at this," she said. She held up a picture of a long-haired boy. "It's Davy Jones, the lead singer for the Monkees. See what I mean? He looks a lot like Ray. Real dreamy, don't you think?"

"I guess," said Pepper, barely glancing at the picture.

Chloe closed the magazine with a snap. "I keep forgetting that you're not a teenager yet."

"You're not that much older than me. Only a few months. Besides, even when I *am* a teenager, I'm not going to be boy crazy like you."

"I'm not boy crazy."

"Yes, you are. You're practically falling all over Ray."

"Am not!"

"Why were you wearing blue eyeshadow when we went to see him the other day?"

"I just felt like trying some of my mom's makeup. It had nothing to do with Ray." Chloe paused for a moment. "Do you think he noticed?"

Pepper shrugged. "How should I know?"

"Did he say anything about me?"

Pepper thought about this. "He said your mom made good jam."

Chloe did not look at all satisfied, so Pepper changed the subject. "Do you want to try that ESP game again? I can try to guess what you're thinking."

Chloe shrugged. "Okay."

Pepper made her mind go blank and waited to see what would pop into her head.

"So, what am I thinking?"

112

"Shhh!" Pepper made her mind go blank again. "You're thinking … you're thinking … you're thinking, when are we going to see Ray again?" she guessed.

"Wrong! I was thinking that I'm going to try some of my mom's new lipstick next time."

Pepper had a feeling that even if she could read Chloe's mind, Chloe would pretend she was wrong, just to be difficult. Besides, there was no point in playing the game with someone who kept yakking the whole time. It was impossible to concentrate.

"Speaking of Ray," Pepper said, "there's something that doesn't make sense to me. Actually, there're a few things." She went on to outline her concerns.

"I'm sure there's a good explanation."

"What could it be?"

"I don't know." Chloe thought for a few minutes. "He seems so nice, but I guess you might be right. He could be lying. He might actually be a criminal. A juvenile delinquent or something. I heard there's a guy who escaped from Brannen Lake. Maybe that's him! I didn't even think about that until now. Did you?"

Pepper didn't want to admit she'd wondered the same thing herself. "No."

"Well, maybe we should. If it turns out he *is* a criminal and we help him, we could be in trouble too."

"Why?"

"I'm pretty sure we'd be … you know … whatchamacallit … accomplices or something like that. We could go to jail too, if anyone finds out."

"Are you sure?"

"Pretty sure. I'd be prepared to bet money on it. Not a lot of money, though. Maybe five bucks."

"What are we betting on? Five bucks he's a criminal, or five bucks we'd go to jail if we were accomplices?"

"I don't have five bucks to bet on anything right now."

"Well, I don't either!"

But the next day Pepper went to see Ray on her own. As soon as Ray let her in the shack, she confronted him. "I've been thinking about you being a draft dodger, and there are a couple of things I don't understand."

Ray's expression turned serious. "Like what?"

Pepper laid out the things that had been troubling her. "You're too young to be drafted. And even if you thought you *might* be drafted, you're in Canada now. You don't need to hide."

Ray nodded slowly. "You're partly right, but there are a few points I should set straight. I'm American like I told you before. Mom had me in the States before she moved up to Canada. I grew up here, and when I'd had enough of foster homes I decided to go back to the States and join the army. A guy can enlist in the army as young as seventeen, but only with his parents' consent. When you get to eighteen, though, you don't need your parents' consent anymore. I'd just turned eighteen, so it was easy."

"What!" Pepper was astounded. "Are you saying you were a soldier?"

"Yes."

"So, it was your choice to join up? You *wanted* to go and fight in a war?"

"I hadn't really thought it through. I wanted to do something that I could be proud of, to make something of myself. I wanted to walk down the street and have people say, There goes a good man." He paused and then laughed softly. "I thought being in the army would be like it is in the movies.

You know, fun, exciting, camaraderie, see the world. But it wasn't like that at all. There were always people yelling at you. Telling you what to do. We had to do stupid drills all day long. And you couldn't talk back or have an opinion of your own. If you did, they made you do an extra ten-mile march through the mud carrying heavy gear."

"So what happened?"

"I never went on a tour of duty. I never even made it through basic training. The drill sergeant had it in for me. One day he told me to do a hundred push-ups for no reason. Just singled me out. The next day, the same thing. A hundred more push-ups. The next day he told me to do it again. I snapped and said some things I shouldn't have. The drill sergeant got all red in the face. He told me to go back to the barracks to cool off. I was supposed to report to the chief officer first thing in the morning. I was in big trouble. I knew that much.

"While I was sitting in the barracks, I got to thinking. I wasn't even sure what the Vietnam War was all about. I didn't know why the Americans were fighting over there. Thousands of innocent people were being killed. Families. Babies. I didn't want any part of that. And I didn't want to get killed, either. But once you're in the army you can't just quit. So I decided I was going to escape."

"How did you do that?" Pepper asked.

"There was a high fence that went all around the base with barbed wire along the top so you couldn't climb over it. On the other side of the fence, you could see the forest. I looked at that forest and wished I could be there. More than anything in the world, that's where I wanted to be."

Pepper shuddered. She knew exactly how he'd felt. She'd dreamed that very thing. "What happened then?"

"There were some workmen at the base doing construction on one of the buildings. They had a bunch of tools lying around. I picked up a pair of pliers and some wire cutters. I scouted out a spot behind the maintenance shop that wasn't too visible. That night I threw my gear in a duffel bag, grabbed my guitar, and cut my way out. I tried to get as far away as I could. I walked all night. I went along the back roads where there wasn't much traffic."

Pepper felt a prickling down her arms, as if her skin was tightening. She knew what he was going to say next.

"If a car came along," Ray said, "I would duck down behind the trees. I thought they might be searching for me." He stopped and looked at Pepper. "Are you okay?"

Another shiver had just passed through her. "Fine," she said. "Keep going."

"When I got far enough away from the base, I decided to take a risk and hitchhike. I caught a ride up the coast to a marina, and I found a fisherman there who said he'd take me across the border to Nanaimo. He charged me for it. A lot. It took every last dollar I had. I thought it would be easier to get through customs at the little fisherman's wharf in Nanaimo than at some of the big border crossings. Turns out it wasn't as simple as I thought."

"What do you mean?"

"Let me explain something. There are draft dodgers and military deserters. The draft dodgers are the ones who leave the country before they ever get drafted into the army. It's a little tricky for them getting into Canada, but most of them make it. The military deserters are the ones who were in the army but then they ran away, like me. In the government's eyes, that's a whole lot worse. If they ever catch you, you're going to jail. You'll be behind bars before you can say 'Yankee doodle dandy.' Canada doesn't want to let in deserters, either.

"When I got to Nanaimo I figured the guy at the border crossing was on to me. He probably had me pegged for a deserter as soon as he saw me. I wasn't wearing my fatigues or my combat boots—I had civilian clothes on—but I had a shaved head, and I probably seemed pretty nervous. I already told you that part of the story, how I had to do some fast talking. But it didn't go quite the way I told you before."

"It didn't?"

"No."

Pepper winced.

Ray put up a hand. "I wasn't looking for trouble. Honest. But he wasn't going to let me into Canada, and when I realized that I made a run for it. The guy grabbed me, and we both went down. I was quicker to get to my feet than he was. I got away and ran a few blocks and hid in an alley. I could hear sirens. I thought they were after me, so I hitch-hiked a ways out of town. I waited in the woods until night, when the tide was low, and I picked this shack 'cause it was off on its own. I pried the plywood off the back window and smashed the glass to get in. That's when I cut my hand." He raised his other hand to display the bandages. "So that's the story. That's why I'm hiding out."

"Aren't you safe now, though? Now that you're actually in Canada?"

"I'm not sure what would happen if I got caught. I'd be in trouble for that scuffle at the border, and now I'm trespassing on private property. That's a couple of laws I've broken, right there." He paused. "If they find me, they might send me right back to the States again."

"Why didn't you tell me the whole truth before?"

"I guess I was worried about what you'd think of me. I know it doesn't sound good." He looked down at the floor and then added quietly, "Bet you never thought you'd have a brother who was wanted on both sides of the border!"

Pepper struggled to take in this new information. It was like the layers of an onion. As soon as she'd grappled with one part of Ray's story, something else came along. "So you're a criminal in both the States and Canada?"

"Well, not exactly. They haven't convicted me of anything in either country. And it's not like I deliberately set out to commit a crime. All along, I've just tried to do what I thought was right. Do you understand?"

"I guess so." Pepper thought for a moment. "You've got to be careful staying here, you know. People notice every little thing. It's like they have eyes in the back of their head. Chloe's mom says, 'If you sneeze, the person in the next shack will say bless you.'"

"I am being careful. The same goes for you too. It's a risk every time you come over here. That's what I've been saying all along."

"Don't worry. I'm always careful. Just one more thing. If you get caught, and they find out I've been helping you, could I go to jail too?"

Ray laughed. "No one's going to send a twelve-year-old to jail."

"Are you one hundred percent sure?"

"Ninety-nine percent."

CHAPTER 10

A Favour

That evening it rained. Pepper, Grandma, and Everett played cards at the kitchen table. The lantern set on the table cast a flickering light around the room. Heavy raindrops drummed on the roof. There was a chill in the air, so Grandma had lit the wood stove. When they finished the last game of Kings in the Corner, Grandma toasted bread with sugar and cinnamon on top before they went to bed.

Pepper couldn't be sure if it was the late-night snack or her troubled thoughts about Ray that made her toss and turn. She finally fell into a restless sleep.

The next morning she woke up feeling groggy. She looked out the window. The clouds were breaking up and the sun was coming out.

"You slept late. It's almost nine," Grandma commented as Pepper emerged from her bedroom cubicle, yawning and rubbing her eyes. "What are your plans for the day?"

"Maybe I'll play with Chloe up at the fort."

"That sounds like a good idea."

Pepper did plan on playing with Chloe, but not right away. She was going to Ghost Island as soon as the tide had gone out far enough.

Everett woke up and came out in his pajamas. His hair was sticking up in all directions.

Grandma set two bowls of steaming porridge down on the table. "Here you go. A good breakfast to start your day. I ate hours ago, and I've already been in for my morning dip." She sat down to finish her tea. "What are you going to do today, Everett?"

"I don't know. Read, I guess."

"Have you met Barry Brewster yet? Maybe you could do something with him."

Everett screwed up his face.

"Pepper's going to her fort to play with Chloe. Why don't you go too?"

Pepper froze, the spoon halfway to her mouth.

"It's a girl's fort," he replied.

"Well, I'll tell you what," Grandma said. "I'll show you how to chop kindling. We're running a bit low so that'll be a real help."

Pepper put the spoon in her mouth and swallowed the porridge. It tasted good. She liked that Grandma put raisins in it.

When Pepper was ready to head out to Ghost Island, she could see Barry hanging around the back of his family's shack. He was tossing up rocks and hitting them with a piece of driftwood like a baseball bat. She waited, but Barry showed no signs of losing interest in his game. She knew if she walked by he'd try to engage her in some annoying conversation. Besides, she didn't want him to see where she was going. Finally he wandered around to the other side of the shack, and she was able to dart by unobserved.

At Ghost Island, Pepper and Ray sat out on the deck. It was still wet from the rain the night before. They'd taken two of the kitchen chairs and set them where they couldn't be seen from the beach. Once they were settled, Pepper asked Ray how long he was planning on hiding out on Ghost Island.

"I've got a plan worked out, and I think it's time. I know someone in Nanaimo. Ajax. He'll help me out. He owes me."

"What do you mean, he owes you?"

Ray hesitated. "It's kind of a long story."

"I don't mind."

"Well, Ajax is kind of a puny kid, and a few years back some guys at school started picking on him. One day they took his leather jacket and were kicking it around the schoolyard like it was some kind of soccer ball. Ajax was standing there watching them. I didn't really know him. I didn't know the other guys, either. But I just knew it wasn't right. So I walked up and grabbed that jacket. I knew those guys were probably scared of me. Every time I changed foster homes I changed schools, and some kids made up stories about me. That I'd been expelled from my last school for fighting. That kind of thing. I never set them straight. Why should I care?" He shrugged. "Anyway, I told those guys if they ever did anything to Ajax again, I was going to come after them. I always kept an eye out for him after that."

"So he's going to help you now?"

"That's right. The night I escaped from the base I called Ajax from a phone booth at a gas station. I told him if I could get across the border, I would lie low for a while. Then, when the time was right, I'd let him know where I was. He said he'd come and get me. He's got some money saved and a car all fixed up. We'll go to Vancouver and track down a group he's heard of. They help people trying to escape the draft, and military deserters too. They know all the rules and how to get around them."

"Are they lawyers?"

"I don't think so, but Ajax says they've got connections with lawyers. I'm hoping they can help me sort this out."

"And then you'll come back? So I can see you again?" Pepper felt a twinge of worry. After all these years of being separated, she and Ray had only just reconnected. They hadn't had nearly enough time to get to know each other yet.

Ray hesitated. "Maybe. I haven't thought too far ahead."

"But you're my brother! We're family."

Ray shifted uncomfortably. "Look, Pepper, I want to be a good brother to you. I really do. But I've got to get myself out of this mess first. I want to be the kind of brother you can be proud of."

"I *am* proud of you."

Ray shook his head. "I'm not proud of myself. Not the way things have turned out. Probably most people wouldn't think much of me right now. A deserter. Hiding from the police. What's there to be proud of?"

"You did what you thought was right. You didn't do things just because other people told you to do them. That's why I'm proud of you. I bet our mom would be proud of you too. And you know what else? I think one day you should go to California and find her."

"I don't know about that, Pepper. I don't know if I'll be

able to go back into the States again. If they find out I'm a deserter, I could go to jail. It's a pretty big risk."

"But you said that group in Vancouver was going to sort everything out for you."

"They might. But let's wait and see what happens. Okay?"

Pepper persisted. "If you were able to find our mom, would you tell her about me?"

"Sure, I would."

"Maybe she'd want to see a picture of me. I could try to find one. And maybe she'd want to write to me. I could give you my address." Pepper chewed her lip as she thought. "And after you found her, you'd come back, right?" She didn't wait for Ray to answer. "Maybe she'd come with you. You could both come and see me in Edmonton. For a visit."

"Yeah. Maybe. But I can't make any promises. Let's say I did decide to go and look for her. First I'd have to get there. Make it across the border without getting caught. It's three or four days of driving to get to California. I'm not even sure Ajax's car would make it. And then who knows if I'd be able to find her."

But Pepper didn't want to hear about all the things that could go wrong. What she wanted, with all her heart, was for Ray to find their mom. "You're going to try, though, right?"

"For you, Pepper, I might. But first I need your help with something. When are you going into town next?"

"Tomorrow. Why?"

"I need you to do me a favour. I want you to call Ajax. This is his number." He wrote it on a piece of paper. "Tell him where I am and ask him to come and pick me up. It's time for me to make a move."

Later that afternoon Pepper and Chloe worked on their fort, adding an extension and hanging some God's-eye decorations they'd made from twigs and brightly coloured yarn.

Chloe suddenly said, "Oh, I almost forgot to tell you. Guess what I heard?"

"What?"

"Redheads have more psychic abilities than other people."

Pepper looked at her in surprise. "Where'd you hear that?"

"My mom. And she heard it from her mom when she was a little girl. I guess people have said that for years and years."

"Psychic abilities … you mean like ESP?"

"Exactly. So you know that ESP game you always want to play? Maybe if you keep practising you'll get really good at it."

For a moment Pepper considered telling Chloe about the strange dreams she'd had. But the dreams were too mysterious. Too private. Too bewildering to put into words.

The next day, Grandma, Pepper, and Everett made a trip into town. When they opened the door to Grandma's house, they found her mail scattered on the mat as usual. There it was—finally!—a letter from home. Grandma opened the envelope and pulled out several pages.

"Looks like there are letters addressed to each of us," she said, handing a page to Everett. "Here's yours, Pepper."

Pepper grabbed it eagerly.

Dear Pepper,

I hope you're having a good time on Shack Island with Grandma. Make sure you mind what she says, and help her with the dishes without having to be asked. She's getting a little older now, and she's not used to looking after two children. Can you remind Everett to help out too? He can chop firewood. Just tell him to be careful with the axe.

The garden is growing well this season. It's been so hot our tomatoes are ripening up faster than we can eat them. I am going to get your dad to help me do some canning this weekend. We've got beans galore.

I've been feeling fine, but I can't do as much as I'd like. I need to have a rest each day and put my feet up. The baby is kicking lots, so it must be healthy. I made a little baby outfit. I had enough leftover material to make a matching hair band for me. Won't that look nice?

Love, Mom

Pepper folded up the letter and shoved it in her pocket. "What does she say?" asked Grandma.

"Just stuff about the garden mostly." Pepper didn't feel like talking. Her mom hadn't said she missed her. And there was nothing from her dad. He hadn't even signed the letter.

Everett spoke up, "In mine she says she's tired all the time, but other than that she's feeling well."

Grandma nodded. "She says that in mine too. She also says she's been making some baby clothes, and she's got a crochet pattern for a baby set she's going to do next. A bonnet, booties, and a little matinee jacket. She's wondering about doing it in mint green. Or maybe yellow."

Pepper forced a sour smile. It felt like the muscles in her cheeks were all cramped up.

Grandma got out her stationery and some pens. "Let's all write back now. We can mail the envelope before we leave for Shack Island."

Pepper sat down at the kitchen table with the others.

Dear Mom and Dad, she wrote. Then she stopped. She looked over at Grandma and Everett. They were scribbling away furiously. She stared at her page, then crossed out *Dear Mom and Dad* and wrote *Dear Colleen and Richard* instead. They weren't her real parents, after all, so why should she call them Mom and Dad? She knew they wouldn't like that, but it was strangely satisfying to write it anyway. She drew a picture of a large starfish, but there was still a lot of white space left on the page, so she wrote,

I've been having an interesting summer, and I met some people I like on Shack Island. My friend Chloe and I made a fort on the bluff. Hope you have a fun time canning beans and making baby outfits.
Pepper

"Are you sure that's all you want to write?" asked Grandma when Pepper handed the letter to her.

"Uh-huh."

Grandma raised her eyebrows, but she said nothing as she folded the page along with hers and Everett's and slid them into an envelope.

Later, when they were all out weeding the garden, Pepper straightened up, stretched her back, and said she had to go inside and get a drink of water. In the kitchen she quickly pulled out the piece of paper Ray had given her, picked up the phone, dialed the number, and counted the rings.

Seven. Eight. Nine. Ten. She was just about to hang up when someone answered.

"Hello?" It was a woman's voice. She sounded middle-aged.

"Hello. Is Ajax there, please?"

"Ajax? No, I'm sorry, he's not. Who's calling?"

"Um—just a friend." What should she say next? Suddenly Pepper felt flustered. "Do you know when he'll be back?" she asked.

"Not exactly. He's out of town. He's got a job planting trees. He might not be back till the end of the summer."

"The end of the summer!"

"Yes. Or longer ... depending on the weather."

Pepper thought fast. "Well, is there a number where I might be able to reach him?"

"Not at the moment. But sometimes he calls home when they go into the nearest town. Do you want me to take a message?"

"No. Thanks." Pepper hated the idea of telling Ray his plan wasn't going to work out. She was about to hang up the receiver when she thought of something. "Wait! If Ajax calls, could you please ask him about the group of people he knows in Vancouver, and how to find them? Tell him Ray wants to know."

"What kind of group is it?"

"Um ... I'm not too sure."

"All right, dear. I'll ask him."

"Thank you very much. I'll phone you back in a week or so to see if he's called. Goodbye." Pepper hung up the phone and wiped her forehead with the back of her hand. It was covered in sweat.

CHAPTER 11

Spider's Web

Pepper had to wait until the following afternoon, when the tide went out, before she could tell Ray that Ajax had left town. Just as she was hurrying by the last few shacks on the main island, she heard someone call out, "Where you going?"

It was Barry Brewster. He'd suddenly swung open the back door of his shack and stepped out onto the step. He was eating some potato chips.

"You've been going over to Ghost Island a lot lately. I've seen you," he continued.

"I'm just going for a walk."

"You've been taking stuff over and leaving it there. Like the other day."

"No. That was just my lunch. Sometimes I eat my lunch over there," Pepper said, and her heart started to pound.

"Maybe I'll go over there today too. See what you're hiding."

"I'm not hiding anything." Pepper kept walking, trying to look as nonchalant as possible. After a few moments she checked over her shoulder and was relieved to see Barry wasn't following her. He was still sitting on the step, intent on getting the last potato chip crumbs out of the bag. Pepper hoped she'd sounded convincing enough to throw him off the scent.

When Pepper gave Ray the bad news that Ajax had left town for the summer, his shoulders slumped and he sank down on the top stair. Pepper sat down beside him.

"Sorry," she said. "I did the best I could."

"I know you did. It's not your fault."

"I asked his mom to try to get the information about the group in Vancouver, though. She's going to ask Ajax if he calls her. I said I'd phone again the next time I'm back in town to see what she found out."

"That was good thinking." He pulled a blade of grass and chewed on it. "That's a long time to wait, though. The longer I stay, the more chance I have of getting caught."

For a moment Pepper wondered if she should mention that Barry had been questioning her. But telling Ray about that would make him want to leave even more. "I don't want you to go," she said. "Please. You're my brother, and we've only just found each other."

"I know that. And it's not a bad set-up. I have a shelter here. You and Chloe are bringing me food." Ray hesitated. "I'll tell you what. I'll take it day by day and see how things go. But I can't make any promises. I might have to leave suddenly. And I don't want you to be disappointed if one day you come by and I'm not here. Do you understand?"

Pepper swallowed hard and nodded.

"But if I'm still here when you talk to Ajax's mom next,

we'll see if she has anything helpful to tell us. If we don't get anywhere with that, I'll have to figure out something else."

Pepper looked sideways at him. She used to think Ray looked a little rough, almost dangerous. But the cut on his hand had healed now. And his hair had grown a bit. Curls were starting to form, catching sunlight like copper. She looked at the freckles on the back of his arms. They were scattered like hundreds of tiny coins across his skin. She liked the way they looked. Like hers.

Then she glanced towards the water and gasped. Barry was halfway along the beach, walking in their direction.

"Quick," she said, grabbing Ray's arm and leaping to her feet. "That's Barry. Get inside before he sees you."

Ray scrambled across the deck. "Who's Barry?"

"A nosy kid from one of the shacks. A troublemaker. No one likes him."

The door shut, and Pepper heard the lock click. She walked down the steps, trying to look as if she had nothing to hide.

"Hey, Barry," she called out.

He squinted at her when he got closer. "Whatcha doing up there?"

"Nothing. Just exploring the island."

"You shouldn't go up on those big rocks, you know. They're dangerous."

Pepper shrugged.

Barry didn't take his eyes off her. "I thought maybe the people who use this place had come for the summer."

"Oh?"

"Yeah. I thought someone was here."

"No. No one's here. Why would you think that?"

He shifted his eyes to the shack, studying it intently.

"I've got my reasons," he said and looked at Pepper.

Pepper met his gaze and held it. She didn't want to be the first to look away.

Finally Barry chuckled and the moment passed. He turned and walked back the way he'd come.

As Pepper watched him go, she felt a sickening wave of worry. What had Barry seen? How much did he know? Was he going to tell anyone?

Or maybe he was only bluffing. It was possible, Pepper told herself. At least she hoped it was. She crossed the fingers on both her hands for luck.

"Barry's getting suspicious," said Pepper later that day as she and Chloe climbed the bank to the car park and started down the road on their way to the store.

"About Ray?"

"Yeah. He followed me over there and was asking a lot of questions."

Chloe shook her head. "You better be careful. If Barry ever found out, he'd turn Ray in."

Pepper's stomach twisted into a knot of panic. Having to keep secrets, and almost getting caught, was making her feel like a fly tangled in a spider's web.

At the store, Chloe pored over the magazines. Her mom had given her enough money to buy one, but she couldn't decide. "*Seventeen. Young Miss. Tiger Beat.* Which one should I get?" She picked up the *Tiger Beat* and leafed through it. "I bet one day Ray could be in a magazine like this. Just watch and see. He's a good enough musician to be famous. And he's got the looks too!" Then she picked up another magazine. "This one's got an article on how to make your hair super shiny. And look. See this?" She shoved a picture of a young woman in a short skirt towards Pepper. "I'm going to ask my mom to hem all my skirts short like this before I go back to school this year."

Pepper picked up a comic book and examined an ad in the back for sea monkeys. One of the sea monkeys in the illustration was wearing a cape and a crown. Maybe she could send away for some. She could get a whole family. She could teach them to do tricks.

Pepper had some money too, though she hadn't told Chloe. She slipped her hand in her pocket and felt the dollar bill she'd taken from the bus envelope. She felt a twinge of recklessness. But if she spent some of her bus money, what would she do when it was time to buy the ticket home? She decided not to think about that. She liked the feeling of possibility and power the dollar bill gave her. She could buy the comic. Or she could buy an ice cream. She could even buy both if she wanted.

"Girls," the lady at the cash register called down the aisle. "This is not a library."

Pepper put the comic back on the rack and turned to Chloe. "Are you going to pick that one? Because if you're not, maybe you could get us ice creams with the money instead. I'd die for an ice cream right now. Wouldn't you? It's so hot. Ice cream with chocolate. Mmmm."

Chloe put her magazine down. "Yeah. That sounds good."

They selected the ice creams from the freezer. As Chloe paid for them, Pepper hung back, feeling a small pang of guilt. But it wasn't enough to stop her from taking the ice cream, blowing into the paper wrapper to unstick it from the frozen chocolate, and closing her eyes to enjoy the first bite. It tasted smooth and cold and luscious, just the way she'd imagined.

Pepper smiled a big, gap-toothed, satisfied smile. "Thanks," she said to Chloe. The dollar bill was still safe in her pocket. She'd return it to the envelope as soon as she got back.

When they reached the car park the tide was already on its way in, running over the pebbles like a river. They took off their runners and sloshed through.

"Good thing we didn't leave it any longer. We would have been stranded over here," said Pepper. The water was already past her ankles.

"We made it just in time," agreed Chloe, struggling to keep her balance on the slippery stones. "Hey! Do you know what I'm thinking right now?"

"No." Pepper was too hot to even bother trying to read Chloe's mind.

"I'm thinking maybe I should have got a magazine after all. Instead of those ice creams."

That night, before Pepper went to sleep, she placed her pen on her apple crate table. She stared at it intently, willing it to move, focusing as hard as she could. Then, amazingly, it began to wobble ever so slightly. It started to roll, picking up speed as it went, and dropped over the edge onto the floor. Pepper could barely believe what had happened. She'd done it! She'd learned to harness her powers of telekinesis.

Pepper was so excited she couldn't sit still. She got up and walked quickly around her little sleeping area, but the space was so small she soon felt dizzy. She sat down on the bed until her head stopped spinning. Then she picked up the pen and put it back on the apple crate. Once again, she focused as hard as she could. The pen wobbled, and then wobbled some more, and then rolled right off the edge.

"Everett!" she called out.

"What?" came his muffled reply from the other side of the purple curtain.

"Look at this."

The curtain shifted, and Everett's face appeared.

Pepper demonstrated how she could make the pen move. When it dropped to the floor the third time, she felt more powerful than ever. She was exultant. She felt like a movie star and the Queen of England all rolled up into one person. If she could move a pen, she thought, imagine what else she could do!

Everett wore an astonished expression at first. Then it turned to doubt. He approached the apple crate with his head cocked to one side. "What's this?" he said as he scooped a sock from the floor where it was stuck under a corner of the crate.

"Oh, that's where my sock went," said Pepper, snatching it from him.

"So much for telekinesis," Everett said. "The crate was crooked. That's why the pen rolled."

Pepper crossed her arms and sat down on the bed with a huff. "You don't have to explain it to me. I can figure it out myself. I'm not stupid!" she said.

After Everett returned to his side of the curtain, Pepper put the pen back on the crate. It remained completely still, exactly where she'd put it.

Several hours later, Pepper's eyes flew open. She sat up, trying to catch her breath. Darkness pressed in around her.

Even though she was awake, her dream did not fade. It felt real. Insistent. Alarming.

Pepper had been rushing down a long hallway. She

was holding a small child by the hand. She wasn't sure if it was a boy or a girl. Every time she turned to check on the child, all she could see was a shadow. Pepper knew she had to hurry, but the child was slowing her down. There were heavy footsteps coming after her. Then she noticed a door partway down the hall. She struggled to turn the doorknob, but the door was locked. The footsteps drew closer. There wasn't much time.

She looked down at the child and realized that it was not a child at all. It was something much smaller, something she held tightly inside her fist. She unfurled her fingers one by one, and there, resting delicately on her palm, was a moth. Its wings were intricately grained, like wood. Two large black eyes on the wings seemed to be looking back at her. The wings pulsed slowly up and down as if marking time. Then, as effortlessly as thistledown floating on a summer breeze, it took flight. It flew through the keyhole of the door and immediately the door swung open.

Pepper darted inside. She slammed the door and leaned all her weight against it. She looked around her. Somehow she was in the shack at Ghost Island. The moth seemed to have disappeared. There was a sudden banging on the other side. Shouting. The door was shaking. Whoever was on the other side was about to come in. And nothing was going to stop them.

CHAPTER 12

The Trouble with Dreams

Pepper's heart beat hard against her ribs. She could not ignore the dream. It was mysterious and frightening, but still very real. She recalled the other strange dreams she'd had that summer—the one about looking through a chain-link fence, the one about running down the road at night, and the other about cutting her hand on glass. All of these things had really happened—to Ray.

Now she had an intense feeling something was about to happen again. Maybe it was happening at this very moment: Ray's hiding place discovered, someone bursting into his shack on Ghost Island. Maybe it was Barry. Or even the police! Yes, the police. That's who it must be, Pepper decided. It was the police who were at Ray's door.

Pepper had to do something. She couldn't stay there, safe in her bed, while Ray was about to be discovered, perhaps even arrested. She threw the blankets back, swung her legs out of bed, and fumbled about in the dark looking for her runners. Then she hesitated. How was she, one girl, going to stop them?

She pushed the curtain aside. "Everett!" she hissed. "Wake up!" She knew Everett wouldn't be much help, but he was her only option at the moment. She had a vague idea that maybe he could talk to the police long enough that she could sneak Ray out of the shack.

Everett stirred groggily. "Wha …?"

"Everett. Hurry. Get out of bed. I need your help."

Everett moaned and sat up. "What's going on?"

"Just put on your shoes. And don't wake up Grandma. We're going outside. I'll tell you on the way."

Once they were outside, Pepper shivered. Her pajamas felt thin against the cold night air. She wished she'd put on a sweater, but there was no time to go back. At least she'd remembered the flashlight. "Come on," she said. She grabbed Everett's arm and dragged him along.

"Where are we going?"

Pepper glanced down the beach. Even though the light of the flashlight did not extend very far, she could see that the tide was low enough that they could cross over on foot.

"This way. The tide's on its way out," urged Pepper. "We're going to Ghost Island."

"Ghost Island? In the middle of the night? What are you, crazy?"

Pepper didn't answer. She had already set off and was well ahead of him.

"Pepper! We better stop and figure out which way the tide is going. It might be on its way in, not out."

Pepper hesitated for a moment but then kept walking. "Try to keep up," she called back over her shoulder.

Everett tagged along reluctantly as Pepper began to explain how she had found Ray and learned that he was her real brother and also an army deserter, and now the police had come to arrest him.

Everett interrupted. "Are you out of your mind, Pepper? It's not logical. First of all, it's highly unlikely that you would find your brother by accident here on Shack Island. In fact, I'd put the odds at a million to one."

"I don't care what the odds are. It happened. I found him. He's my brother, and that's that."

"If he's a deserter, he could be in a lot of trouble. And you could be too, for associating with him. I think we should turn around right now."

"I'm not turning around. I'm going to Ghost Island. Even if you aren't." Pepper kept walking.

"Oh, all right! I'll go with you. But only because I don't want you going over there by yourself." He hurried to catch up with her again. As they walked through the night, Everett kept bombarding her with questions. "How do you know he's your brother?" "Why haven't you told anyone?" "We're going over there because you had a dream?"

"It wasn't an ordinary dream," Pepper explained. "It was one of my ESP dreams. I've had them before. And they've all turned out to be true."

"ESP! I keep telling you that's a bunch of baloney."

"No, it's not. Hurry up, will you? There's no time to lose." All Pepper could think about was saving Ray.

At the stairs leading up from the beach, Pepper and Everett crouched down. The shack was quiet. Had the police gone inside already? Pepper inched up the stairs. Everett lagged behind. She tried the door. It was locked.

138

She knocked. There was no sound from inside. She knocked louder.

"There's no one there," said Everett over the knocking.

"I bet there is. The police must have forced their way in." She banged on the door as hard as she could.

Everett grabbed Pepper by the shoulders. "Stop! Don't you see? The door hasn't been forced open. The lock isn't damaged. You just had a bad dream. We've got to go now, before the tide starts to come in."

Pepper pushed Everett's hands away. It was true. The lock had not been damaged. There was no sign of forced entry. But maybe Ray had opened the door himself. Or maybe the police had got in through the broken window at the back.

"We've come this far. We've got to make sure he's okay," Pepper insisted as she stumbled through the bushes to the back window.

"What are you doing now?" called Everett.

Pepper didn't bother to answer. She hoisted herself up and scrambled over the sill. The inside of the shack was completely dark. Pepper wished she hadn't left the flashlight on the ground outside. Inside the shack there was no sound. All she could hear was her own ragged breathing. But the police might be in the shadows, waiting.

She felt her way across the kitchen to the door and unlocked it. "Everett. Grab the flashlight. This way."

Everett entered cautiously. He shone the flashlight side to side. Kitchen chairs, the table, the cupboards, were illuminated one after the other. There was no sign of anyone.

"Look in the bedroom," ordered Pepper. "You go first."

Everett approached the bedroom door. It was half open. The flashlight lit up a corner of the room. Everett reached forward and swung the door the rest of the way open.

Ray was sitting bolt upright in the middle of the bed, staring straight at them. In the next instant he leapt up and hurled himself at Everett, throwing him to the floor. The flashlight skittered across the floorboards, leaving the two struggling boys in darkness. Pepper heard the sounds of punching and grunting.

"Stop! Ray!" she called out. "It's me, Pepper."

The struggle stopped abruptly. "Pepper?" It was Ray's voice. "What are *you* doing here?"

"I came to save you from the police. I thought they were coming to arrest you." She retrieved the flashlight and shone it in Ray's direction. He had Everett pinned to the floor. Everett's glasses had been knocked off.

Ray looked at Everett's face. "Who's this guy?"

"Everett. He's my brother. From my adoptive family."

"What the—Pepper! You're not supposed to tell anyone I'm here!"

"I know. I know."

"First you told Chloe. And now you've told your brother."

"I was just trying to protect you," said Pepper huffily. "I thought he might be able to help."

"No offence," said Ray with a nod towards Everett, "but he's not much of a fighter."

Everett just rubbed his shoulder and winced.

Ray turned back to Pepper. "Have you told him everything? About me, I mean?"

Pepper nodded.

"Oh, man …" Ray shook his head slowly, stood up, and brushed himself off. Everett rolled over on his side and groaned. "Sorry, buddy," said Ray, offering Everett a hand to sit up and passing him his glasses. "I heard all this banging and voices at the door, and it was dark. Suddenly there was a light shining in my face, and I couldn't see who it was."

"You thought it was the police, didn't you?" said Pepper. "Yeah."

"Sorry," she said. Pepper looked first at Ray and then at Everett. "I made a mistake."

Everett dragged himself up off the floor and sat down on a chair. "I'll say." His hair was dishevelled, and he looked upset.

Ray sat down too. "What possessed you to come over here in the middle of the night like that? You scared the bejeezus out of me."

"Well ... I had a dream. It seemed real." Pepper couldn't begin to explain how this dream, like the others, had been much more than a dream.

"Pepper, when are you going to learn?" said Everett. "Look at the mess you got me into. Dragging me out in the middle of the night to get beaten up by some kind of ... hobo." ·

"He's not a hobo. He's a deserter."

"What difference does it make? He still beat me up."

"I already said I was sorry."

"Look," interjected Ray. "I know what you're thinking, Everett. You're thinking I'm nothing but trouble. You're thinking your sister better steer clear of me. That I can't be trusted. That someone should turn me in, because that's what I deserve. That's what you think. Isn't it?"

Everett didn't answer.

"Well, isn't it? Isn't that what you're thinking?"

"I guess."

"And I don't blame you. I'd think the same thing the first time I met someone like me. But the truth is, I'm not

141

a bad person. I'm not that different from you. I just made a couple of mistakes along the way. You can understand that, can't you?"

Everett gave a tentative nod.

"Pepper's my sister too. I want to be a good brother to her. I want to look out for her, just like you. When she was a little girl I looked after her. I did my best for her. I would have cut off my right arm for her. And that's the way I still feel. Look, if I met a guy like me, I'd have my doubts at first too. You're smart, Everett, and I respect that. But we both know it takes a while to see a person's true character, to figure out if a person's decent or not. I'm not asking you to do me any favours. All I'm asking is for you to give me a chance. Okay? Don't tell anyone I'm here. Give it a day or two, and see what you think. Will you do that?"

Everett shifted uncomfortably in his chair. "Well, okay," he said reluctantly.

Ray extended a hand, and Everett shook it.

Then, suddenly, Everett jumped up. "The tide!" he said. "We weren't sure if it was on its way in or its way out. We better go."

All three rushed down the stairs in the dark. The pebbly beach was difficult to run across. The stones shifted beneath their feet, and a cold night wind buffeted them. Pepper had a terrible feeling it was too late. As she ran she could hear that the waves were much closer than they had been before. Then cold water was lapping at her feet. Her runners were soaked through. There was no doubt about it. The tide had come in, and they were stuck on Ghost Island.

Pepper groaned loudly. "What are we going to do now?"

"It won't be low tide again until tomorrow afternoon," said Everett. He began pacing anxiously back and forth.

"But we have to get back before Grandma wakes up and sees we're gone!"

"What about a boat? Ray, is there a boat here on the island?" asked Everett.

"No," said Ray. "A boat would have come in handy for me, but I've looked all over the place. If the people who own this shack ever had one, they must have taken it with them."

Pepper felt desperate. "What if we swim back?"

"Don't even think about it, Pepper," said Everett. "We'd drown on a night like this. It's pitch black. The waves are high. And it's a lot farther than you'd think."

"Everett's right," said Ray. "Even in the daylight on a calm day I'd think twice about it. You'd have to be a strong swimmer to make it."

Pepper felt so frustrated she thought she was going to cry. Everett and Ray were probably both mad at her now. If only she'd ignored her dream, none of this would have happened. Everett wouldn't have found out about Ray. They wouldn't have barged in on Ray, practically scaring him to death. And they wouldn't have ended up stranded on Ghost Island.

"It's all your fault," said Everett. "I could be in my bed asleep right now, if it wasn't for you."

"Shut up," Pepper said and sniffed loudly. "You don't have to tell me."

Ray put an arm around Pepper's shoulder. "Come on. Let's not fight about it. We can go back inside. There's nothing you can do now but wait until morning."

Ray insisted Pepper have the bed. He pulled out a cot and unfolded it in the kitchen for Everett.

"What about you?" Pepper asked Ray.

"The floor's good enough for me," he said. "It won't bother me one bit."

143

Pepper had a warm woollen blanket and a pillow, but she couldn't settle. Troubled thoughts raced around in her head. What was Grandma going to do in the morning when she discovered they weren't there? Maybe she'd think they'd woken up and gone out extra early. No, there was no chance of that. Grandma was always the first one up. Most mornings she'd have had her ocean dip, dressed, and made herself a cup of tea, all before they'd even opened their eyes. Pepper rolled over and tried to think about other things. But she couldn't stop worrying. Once Grandma realized they were gone, how much trouble were they going to be in? What excuse could they make for going to Ghost Island in the middle of the night?

Oh, how foolish she'd been to trust a silly dream! It had steered her wrong. She'd let everyone down. There was no doubt about it; she'd made a great big mess of things.

But Pepper kept coming back to one idea. In some strange way, the dream had ended up coming true. Ray had woken up thinking the police were at the door, even though it had only been Pepper and Everett making the noise.

Pepper slept fitfully, tossing and turning the rest of the night. It felt like the longest night of her life.

"Do you want something to drink?"

Pepper opened one eye and then the other. For a moment she couldn't think where she was. Then, with a terrible sinking feeling, it all came back to her.

Ray stood in the doorway holding a mug. "It's Freshie. It's all I have."

Pepper sat up. Her head ached. "What time is it?" The room was in deep shadow. A single shaft of pale light edged past the plywood window covering.

"Almost ten. Everett's already up." He passed her the mug.

Ten! Pepper drank the unnaturally sweet orange drink in one gulp, then threw back the covers. "We better get down to the beach before anyone comes looking for us. If they find us here, they'll find you too," she said.

Everett came to the bedroom door. He looked like he hadn't slept at all. His hair stuck out on one side and lay flat on the other. "It's high tide right now. We still can't walk across."

When Ray let them out, he gave Everett a pat on the back and winked at Pepper. "Good luck," he said and closed the door behind them.

"What are we going to tell Grandma?" Pepper wondered as they went down the stairs to the beach.

"I've been thinking about that. Let's just say we wanted to see if there really was a ghost on Ghost Island, and then we got caught by the tide."

"Okay. That sounds good." Pepper felt relieved. At least they'd have the same story.

Across the water, they could see a few people walking up and down the beach on the main Shack Island. Pepper and Everett shouted and waved. One man stopped, shielded his eyes, looked in their direction, and then called over someone else. A woman wearing a floppy hat and Bermuda shorts joined the man. Pepper recognized the outfit immediately. It was Grandma. Grandma waved and called out something, but they were too far away to hear the words.

Pepper watched as Grandma and a couple of the others carried a rowboat down to the water's edge. Then Grandma got in and rowed across.

"What are you two doing over here?" she said crossly

when her boat ran up on the gravel. "I've been beside myself with worry looking for the pair of you. I've been up since dawn."

Pepper hung her head. "Sorry."

Everett cleared his throat. "We wanted to see if there really was a ghost on Ghost Island. We didn't think we'd get caught by the tide."

Grandma looked sharply at each one of them. "A ghost! You were looking for a ghost?"

Pepper and Everett nodded.

"Well, of all the foolish things I've ever heard! What made you want to do that?"

Everett nudged Pepper in the ribs with his elbow, and Pepper spoke up. "I wanted to find out for myself last night. But I was too scared to come over here on my own, so I made Everett come with me."

Grandma made a tsk-tsk sound with her tongue. "Why didn't you let me know you were going out in the middle of the night?"

"We didn't want to wake you up. And we thought we'd only be gone a short time."

"You could have left a note. Do you have any idea how worried I was?"

"Sorry," Everett and Pepper said together.

"Well, get in and put on your life jackets," Grandma said. "I think that's about enough shenanigans for one day."

Halfway back, Grandma stopped rowing for a few seconds. "The next time we go into town, I'd like you both to weed the whole garden. I think that's only fair, don't you?"

When Grandma started rowing again, Everett looked at Pepper and made a face.

Pepper pretended not to see.

146

CHAPTER 13
Moon Landing

"Shhh. Everyone, quiet, please! I think something's happening." Everett leaned over his transistor radio and turned up the volume. His hands were shaking with excitement.

The announcer's voice on the radio sounded tinny. "Today, July 20, 1969, history is being made. The NASA lunar module, the *Eagle*, has landed. We are expecting very shortly to hear that Neil Armstrong will be stepping onto the surface of the moon."

Earlier in the day, Everett had pleaded with Grandma to go in to town so they could watch the very first moon walk on television. But Grandma, still upset by the events of the day, was in no mood to humour him. She said she wasn't going to waste gas driving in to town any more than she had to. Besides, she'd reasoned, they would be able to hear everything perfectly fine on the radio.

Now the three of them were crowded around the kitchen table in the cabin.

147

"The exact location on the lunar surface is the Sea of Tranquility ...," the radio announcer was saying.

"The Sea of Tranquility?" Pepper said. "How are they going to walk in the Sea of Tranquility? They should call it a lunar swim!" She could feel a pig snort coming on.

"It's only *called* a sea," Everett said, casting an annoyed look her way. "Everyone knows there's no water on the moon. The Sea of Tranquility is really a huge crater that was formed when a giant asteroid smashed into the moon."

Pepper was not put off. She snorted loudly and continued, "Maybe they're going to see little green men rowing around in tiny green boats, and crystal houses and alien spaceships." Although Pepper said this mostly to tease Everett, she actually thought it was possible that the astronauts would find some form of life on the moon. After all, UFOs had to come from somewhere.

Everett didn't even smile. He just turned up the volume on the radio.

The radio voice continued. "Any moment now, we are hoping to hear news that astronauts Neil Armstrong and Buzz Aldrin will be emerging from the module for their moon walk."

"They've been saying that for hours. How long has it been since they landed?" Pepper said in a loud whisper.

"Six hours. Now, shhh. *Some* people are trying to listen."

"But what can they be doing in there all this time?"

"Preparations. Shhh ..."

Pepper slapped a mosquito on the back of her arm. The only excitement she'd felt in the past few hours was when the radio batteries ran out and the shack was turned upside down in a mad scramble to find new ones.

The radio crackled and buzzed as Everett adjusted the antennae. They could hear the radio transmissions between Houston, the command module *Columbia*, and Tranquility base. They heard the voices of the astronauts all the way from the moon and the beeps that signalled the end of each transmission. Pepper caught the occasional phrase, but she was tired of listening.

Then she heard, "Open the hatch when we get to zero ..." "Hatch is coming open."

Pepper sat up and paid attention. She leaned in closer to the radio. Any minute now a man would walk on the moon. It seemed impossible to believe. Until that moment, the moment when the lunar module's door opened, the magnitude of the event had not struck her. Now she could barely stand waiting. The minutes stretched out. What was taking them so long? The radio announcer was talking on and on, recapping the hours, the days that had led up to this moment.

"Now, you're clear ..." "Okay, Houston. I'm on the porch ..." "All systems go ..." "We're getting a picture on the TV ..." "Okay, Neil. We can see you coming down the ladder now ..." "Pretty good little jump ..." "I'm at the foot of the ladder ..." "The surface appears to be very, very fine grained ... almost like a powder ..."

There was a crackle and a hiss, and then, very clearly, they heard Neil Armstrong say, "That's one small step for man, one giant leap for mankind."

The little group broke into a jubilant cheer. They were dancing around the kitchen, hugging each other.

Pepper looked at Everett. For the first time in her life, she saw tears streaming down his face.

A little later, when it was just starting to get dark, Pepper went outside and almost tripped over Barry, who was sitting on the Periwinkle's stairs.

"What are you doing here?" she demanded. "Spying?"

"No!" Barry scrambled to his feet and stalked off.

How long had he been sitting there? she wondered. What a creepy kid! She walked along the beach and back again, then sat down to wait for the moon to come up. It rose—a luminous crescent in a velvety sky. How amazing to think that people were actually up there! Then she looked over towards Ghost Island. She couldn't see it, but she knew it was there, somewhere in the darkness. She thought back to last night's disastrous visit. Her cheeks burned at the memory. Now he was over there all by himself. Maybe he was looking at the moon too at this very moment. He might be thinking how beautiful it was. But he would have no way of knowing the moon landing had been successful. He would have missed the whole thing.

The moon landing was exhilarating, daring, and inspiring. Pepper longed to do something just as exciting. And that's when the idea came to her. It would be risky. So risky, in fact, that at first she didn't think it would be possible. But she couldn't help wondering if there might be some way to make it work. It made her heart speed up just thinking about it. No. It was too crazy. The sensible thing to do was to forget the whole notion. She tucked the idea into the darkest corner of her mind, as firmly and deliberately as closing a door.

The next day Pepper noticed that Everett seemed distracted. He'd read a page of his science magazine, get up and pace around for a while, and then go back to the same page as if he'd never read it before. Finally, late in the afternoon, he left the shack with Grandma's binoculars. He went along the beach and sat down before training them on the point of land where April lived. Pepper snuck up behind him.

"Why don't you just go over there and talk to her?" she said.

Everett jumped. "Who?"

"April, that's who. I know you like her."

He opened his mouth to speak and then closed it again. His cheeks flushed a telltale red. "I don't know if she'd even remember me."

"Sure she would. I bet she'd like it if you went over to see her." Pepper hoped this would boost his confidence. Being geeky was one thing, but being a geek with no confidence was even worse.

"You do?" He chewed his lip. "I've been thinking about it ever since I woke up this morning. Do you know what? I think I'm going to do it."

"You should."

"She's there right now, by the pool. But ... but I wouldn't know what to say to her."

Just then Barry walked by. He eyed the binoculars and cocked an eyebrow. Then he made a chicken sound.

"Shut up, Barry," snapped Pepper.

Barry laughed. "I've told you before, Everett. You're wasting your time going after a girl like April. She wouldn't give you a second look if you were the last—"

"I told you to shut up," Pepper interrupted. "No one cares what you think."

After Barry had walked off, Pepper turned back to Everett. "Don't pay any attention to him. He's just weird. Did I tell you I caught him hanging around outside our place last night?"

"What did he want?" A nervous look passed across Everett's face.

"I don't know. And I don't care." Pepper sat beside him. "Are you still going over to April's?"

He shook his head. "Maybe tomorrow."

Just from the way he said it, Pepper knew he wasn't going tomorrow, either. Sometimes she wished she could take him by the shoulders and give him a good shake.

"Well, the tide's out. We could sneak over and see Ray," she said finally. "We could take him some food. I've got some stuff I've stored under my bed."

"I'm not sure about Ray ..."

"Come on, Everett. We've got to help him. He's my brother!"

"Think of all the trouble we got into the other night when we went there."

"Well, even if you don't want to help him, *I'm* going to."

"I don't think it's a good idea for you to keep going over there. In fact, I think we should tell someone about him. Maybe even the police."

"No! Don't do that."

"At least we should tell Grandma."

"Definitely not. Besides, if we tell Grandma, she'll know we were lying before about why we spent the night on Ghost Island." Pepper paused. She could see Everett considering this. Before he could say anything else, she continued, "You only met Ray once. When you get to know him you'll see he's all right." Pepper stood up. "I'm going over there. Are you coming or not?"

"Okay, okay." Everett stood up too. "But only because you're being so pig-headed about it. I don't want you getting into a dangerous situation. But let's not be too obvious, and this time let's make sure we get back in time."

Ray was sitting on the bottom step whittling a piece of wood. As Pepper came closer, she saw the wood was carved into the shape of a bird. She hoped he had carved it for her. But Ray slipped the bird into his pocket. "Hey, strangers," he said, greeting them with a big grin. He'd eaten all of his food, so he looked eagerly through the items they'd brought. Then he stuffed two slices of bread into his mouth at the same time.

"Thanks," he said with his mouth full. After he'd swallowed, he turned to Everett. "It's good to see you, buddy. I'm sorry we got off on the wrong foot. How are you doing?"

"I'm doing okay. Still got a couple of bruises."

"Did the two of you get in trouble when you got back?"

Pepper told him how Grandma was going to make them weed the whole garden.

Ray laughed. Then he noticed the binoculars hanging around Everett's neck. "Whatcha been doing with those?"

Everett didn't answer.

"He's been looking at a girl," offered Pepper, and then she bit her tongue. Everett shot her a nasty look.

Ray raised his eyebrows. "A girl? Nothing wrong with that. What's her name?"

"April," said Everett.

"She your girlfriend?"

"No."

"But you like her, though. Right?"

"Yeah. I guess."

Pepper spoke up again. "He won't go and talk to her. He says he's going to, but then he doesn't."

Everett shot her another nasty look.

"Fine," said Pepper with a sniff. "I know when I'm not wanted. You two go ahead and talk without me. I'm going up to the shack." She stomped up the stairs and banged the door shut. Then she opened it quietly again and tiptoed back to the top of the stairs. Below her the two boys were talking.

"I don't know what to say to her," Everett said. "She's not going to be interested in someone like me. I'd end up being a laughingstock. Everyone would make fun of me."

"Who's going to know?"

"Well, April for one. You. Me. Pepper. Oh, and Barry."

"Barry? That nosy kid?"

"That's the one. And he's not just nosy; he's a bully too. He's always giving me a hard time."

Ray nodded. "You want to know what I think?"

"Sure."

"All right. I can tell you something about girls, and I can tell you something about bullies. It's kinda the same for both of them. Here's what you do. Never let them know you're scared. You gotta show some confidence. A little confidence goes a long way."

"But I don't have any confidence."

"That's the trick. You don't really have to. You just have to pretend you do. Kinda like acting, you see?"

"Maybe it works for some people, but not for me. I wouldn't be any good at acting."

"Ah! That's where you're wrong. Anyone can learn to do it. I'll give you a few tips. With Barry, this is what you do. You gotta stand up straight. You gotta look him in the eye. You gotta talk like every word you say is important." He paused. "That means no mumbling, right?"

154

"Right."

"What? I didn't hear you."

"Right!"

"That's better. Talk like you mean it. You're in control. Got it?"

Everett nodded.

"It's the same with girls. It's the same three rules. Stand tall. Look 'em in the eye. Talk like you got the world by the tail. Now ... let me have a look at this girl of yours. Let's see what we're dealing with."

"I don't know if you can see her from here," said Everett. He put the binoculars up to his eyes and dialed the focus. "Oh, yeah, there she is. She's still there."

"Let's see." Ray took the binoculars. "I just see an old lady. Looks like she's painting a picture."

"No. That's my grandma. Look past her, over to the shore on the far side. And more to the right."

Ray scanned the landscape. Then he stopped. He took a good long look. "That's her? By the pool? In an orange bathing suit?"

"Yeah."

Ray took another long look. Then he passed the binoculars back. "Well, I can see why she caught your eye."

"So, I just have to do what you said?"

"Hmmm ... maybe you need something else. A girl like that, she's going to have all sorts of guys buzzing around her like bees 'round a hive. You gotta do something that makes you stand out from the rest."

"Like what?"

Ray thought for a moment. "Give her this. Say you made it for her." He pulled the piece of wood he'd whittled out of his pocket and handed it to Everett.

Pepper was dismayed. She wanted the bird, but she knew better than to speak up. They'd know she'd been eavesdropping.

Everett turned the carving over. "Where'd you learn to carve like this?"

Ray shrugged. "It's just something I picked up along the way. There's not a heck of a lot to do around here."

"Thanks. But do you think she'll believe I carved this?"

Ray chuckled. "Why not? Give it to her, and remember the three rules. You'll be a shoo-in."

After supper the following day, Chloe and Pepper sat in their fort with the binoculars, watching for Everett to return from April's.

"Let's see how he looks when he comes back," said Pepper. "We'll be able to tell how it went just by looking at him."

"I wonder how long we'll have to wait?" said Chloe.

"It might be a while."

"Or it could be really quick, if he bombs."

"Don't say that! Besides, I thought you said he was cute before."

"Well, in a way he is. But not like Ray."

Pepper rolled her eyes.

Chloe reached into her pocket for some gum. "Want some? It's Dubble Bubble." She tore it in two and offered a piece to Pepper. She popped the other piece in her mouth as she read the comic. "This is dumb."

"Let me see." Pepper read the comic and crumpled it up. "That's so funny, I forgot to laugh."

"Told you." Chloe blew a bubble so big it popped. Then

she said, "Have you ever noticed that whenever you see Barry he's always by himself?"

"That's because he's a great big jerk. No one wants to be with him."

Chloe chewed her gum thoughtfully. "It's still kind of sad, though, when you think about it." Then she perked up. "You know how I wanted to try some makeup on you before? You should let me try. Just a little bit."

"I don't want any makeup," Pepper said. The last thing she wanted was to look like a clown with blue eyeshadow.

"Come on, I could make you look really cute. I could borrow my mom's new lipstick. It's hot pink."

"No."

"Maybe you're right. With your colouring, tangerine might be better …"

Pepper stopped listening. Everett hadn't come right back, which had to be a good sign. She chewed her wad of gum until it was soft and tried to blow bubbles. She looked at the way the sun glinted off the tiny hairs on the back of her arm, and scratched a mosquito bite on her ankle. She watched a dragonfly circling closer and closer. She held very still. It came so close she could almost feel the beating of its wings. Then, in the next instant, it flew off.

Chloe was still talking. "… and a miniskirt right up to about here, a pair of go-go boots, and maybe some patterned tights instead of those plaid pedal-pushers you're always wearing—"

"What's wrong with them?" Pepper interrupted. She wasn't going to admit she didn't like them either.

"Everything! Too long. Too baggy. And the colours make me want to gag."

"My mom made them."

"Well, *excuse me!* Look, I'm not trying to be mean. I'm trying to help. Maybe you should let me cut your hair. I've never cut hair before, but I think I'd be quite good at it. I was thinking something with a bit more of a bang, and …"

Pepper suspected Chloe would keep talking even if no one was there. Finally she'd had enough. "Chloe, if you think I'm so square, how come you hang around with me?"

Chloe looked surprised. Several seconds passed before she spoke again. "You know why I hang around with you? Simple. 'Cause I like you. I don't have to worry what you think about me. I can just be myself. Even if I say something stupid, or do something stupid, it doesn't matter. I know you're still going to be my friend. That's why."

Pepper wasn't expecting such a heartfelt answer. Before she could think what to say, Chloe continued, "Besides, the next time we go to the store, you owe me an ice cream."

That made them both laugh.

"I could go for an ice cream right now," said Pepper.

"Me too!"

"It's too hot to walk all the way to the store today, though." Pepper picked up the binoculars and looked through them again. Still no Everett. She scanned across to the other side of the island. Three people carrying bags and boxes were walking down from the car park. She'd never seen them before. "Look," she said, passing Chloe the binoculars. "Who are they?"

Chloe took one look and her mouth gaped open. "Oh, no! They're the family who live on Ghost Island. We've got to warn Ray before they get there!"

They skidded down the hill, sending pebbles skittering along the path ahead of them. Then they raced past the row of shacks and across the wet rocks to Ghost Island.

CHAPTER 14
Topsy-Turvy

Pepper cast a glance over her shoulder as they ran. "That family is still a ways back."

"They're probably going slow because they're carrying all that stuff," Chloe said, huffing and puffing.

When they got to the shack, the girls ran up the stairs and pounded at the door. "Quick!" Pepper cried out when Ray opened it. "The owners are coming. We've gotta get you out of here."

They scurried through the shack, putting things in order and grabbing Ray's few possessions. Chloe checked outside. "They're halfway across!"

"You girls go out the door. I'll lock it behind you and climb out the back window."

"As soon as they see the broken window, they're going to know someone's been here," said Pepper.

"Go. There's no time to argue," said Ray as he pushed her out the door.

A few seconds later Ray scrambled out the window. The rocky bluff behind the shack was too steep to climb. There was no other place to hide, so the three of them crouched down behind the shack and waited.

"As soon as they go inside, that's our cue. We'll have to sneak along the rocks, climb down to the beach, and start running," whispered Ray.

"Shhh. I think they're coming."

They heard footsteps coming up the stairs. There was talking and laughing, the sounds of the bags being dumped on the deck and the key in the lock.

Pepper poked her head around the corner. The people had gone inside.

"Now!" she mouthed.

Ray, Chloe, and Pepper scurried away from the shack, clambered down the rocks to the beach, and broke into a run.

"Do you think they saw us?" asked Chloe when they got to the main island.

"I don't know," said Pepper.

Ray was ahead of them. He'd reached a tangle of washed-up logs, stuffed his guitar case between a couple of logs, and jumped down out of sight. Pepper and Chloe sank onto a log beside him. They were all panting to catch their breath.

"Now what?" said Pepper.

"We can't stay here," Chloe said. "People walk up and down here all the time. Look! There's someone right now. Stay down, Ray."

A figure was walking towards them from the far end of the beach. Ray crouched farther down between the logs, but his white T-shirt and the sunburned skin at the back of his neck were still visible. Pepper and Chloe sat on the log in front, hoping to create a screen. They pretended to be sifting through the sand looking for seashells.

Pepper could feel her muscles knotting up with tension. She was ready to get up and run at a moment's notice. She glanced anxiously at the approaching figure. Then she recognized him. Her muscles relaxed, and she waved him over. "It's only Everett."

Everett was surprised when he saw Ray hiding behind the logs. "What are you all doing here?"

Pepper explained how they had escaped from Ghost Island in the nick of time. "But now we have no place for Ray to hide out," she finished.

"It's about time for me to move on anyway," Ray said. "I can't stay here forever."

"Don't go yet," said Pepper. "Maybe we can find you a new place."

"I know!" Chloe said suddenly. "There's a shack on the far side of Middle Island. The rocky side. It's all on its own. I don't think anyone's been there all summer. At least not so far."

Ray hesitated. "Well, I guess we could have a look. But we better do it now, before the tide turns."

As they headed towards Middle Island, a couple of men fixing a roof on one of the shacks looked up and waved.

"There's Bus and Mr. English. Act natural. Just keep walking. If we don't go now, we'll miss our chance," whispered Chloe, waving back.

They stayed as close to the water's edge as they could, clumped together, hoping Ray didn't stand out.

The men went back to their hammering.

It was a scramble to reach the shack, which was on the

isolated side of the island, facing the open ocean. Waves crashed on the rugged shore. The approach was treacherous. A huge rock, split in two, provided a narrow entrance to the remote spot. They squeezed through, one at a time.

Ray skirted the small building, looking it over with a practised eye. He picked up a sturdy stick, wedged it under one of the boards covering the window, and levered the stick back and forth until a few of the nails gave way with a noisy squawk. Then he wrenched the board free from the window frame. He tried to open the window but it wouldn't budge, so he picked up a rock and smashed the glass. He brushed the glass off the sill, hoisted himself up, and wiggled inside. A moment later he opened the door.

"Welcome," he said with a grin. The entire process had taken less than five minutes.

Chloe and Everett went inside, but Pepper hung back. Everything felt topsy-turvy. One minute Ray had been safely hidden away on Ghost Island, and the next minute he'd almost been discovered. Something else was bothering Pepper as well. Part of her felt relieved that Ray had a new hiding spot, but another part felt shaken. Smashing a window, breaking in, trespassing—it suddenly felt very wrong. A crime, in fact. She knew Ray had broken the law before, but somehow she had not been faced with the reality of it until now.

Ray was still standing in the doorway. "Well, are you coming in or not?"

Pepper felt a strong desire to turn and run away, but she forced her feet to go inside.

It was a smaller shack than the one on Ghost Island. The air was stale and musty. The kitchen shelves held only a few items: some cans of corn, a box of baking soda, and a jar of peanut butter. There were a table and chairs, and a mousetrap in the corner with a piece of hardened orange cheese. In the back of the shack they found a bed with a pillow and blankets.

"Couldn't be better," said Ray, throwing himself down on the mattress and putting his hands behind his head. "Chloe, you did well to think of this place."

Pepper went outside again and sat on the step in the sunshine. She took several deep breaths of the fresh air and watched the waves crash against the rocks. A few minutes later Chloe came out and sat down beside her.

Inside the cabin they could hear the boys talking.

"So, how's it going with that girl of yours?" they heard Ray say.

Pepper started. She'd almost forgotten. Only an hour ago she and Chloe had been up at the fort, watching for Everett's return. So much had happened since then, it felt like days had passed.

"Pretty good, I guess," she heard Everett say. "I gave her the bird carving."

"Great. Did you remember the three rules?"

"Sort of. A bit. That stuff doesn't come naturally to me, like it does to you."

Chloe caught Pepper's eye. "Sounds like he bombed," she whispered.

"Don't worry. It'll get easier," Ray told Everett. "You just need a little practice. Once you get your confidence, the girls will be falling all over you."

"Do you really think so?"

"Are you kidding me? You're smart. You're a nice guy. Believe me, you've got a lot going for you."

After a minute, Pepper heard the sound of Ray's

guitar. Ray didn't sing this time. He simply played a melody so beautiful it made Pepper forget everything she'd been worrying about. Even the waves and the wind seemed to stop to listen. At the end of the song, she heard Everett say, "Do you think you could teach me to play like that?"

"Sure," said Ray. "Here, hold the guitar like this ..."

The next time they went into town with Grandma, Pepper secretly made another phone call to Ajax's mother.

"Have you heard from Ajax?" Pepper asked her.

"No, dear, I haven't talked to him. If he called, I must have missed him. I'm sorry."

"All right, then. Thanks anyway." Pepper hung up the phone, groaned loudly, and banged her forehead several times against the wall.

"Is something wrong?" Grandma had suddenly appeared at the back door.

Pepper straightened up quickly. "No. Nothing. Just a bit of a headache."

"Well, no wonder. I'd have a headache too if I was banging my head against the wall like that."

CHAPTER 15

Words So Sweet

Pepper had not seen Ray for several days. She'd gone to his cabin the day before and knocked and knocked, but there'd been no answer. She felt a niggle of worry. Had he finally decided it was too risky to stay on Shack Island and left? No, surely he would tell her if he was going.

In one small way, though, Pepper had felt relieved he wasn't there yesterday. She didn't have to tell him there still was no news from Ajax. And she could put it off again today, because Grandma had decided to take Pepper fishing. By the time she and Grandma got back, the tide would be in again and she wouldn't be able to walk over to Middle Island.

"Why don't you try rowing?" suggested Grandma, once they'd pushed the boat off.

Pepper had never rowed a boat before. The oars kept angling off in different directions. They wouldn't stay in the oarlocks. Sometimes they only skimmed the surface of the

165

water. And it was difficult to get used to facing backwards. She had to keep turning around to see where she was going.

"Rowing is a lot harder than it looks," said Pepper. Already her shoulders were aching.

Grandma laughed. "You've got to keep at it. Everett was like you when he started, and now he's a fine rower."

Pepper kept trying. Eventually she was able to manoeuvre the boat out into the bay. They bobbed in the water near the kelp beds.

"This is a good spot," said Grandma. "Let's switch positions so you can try fishing now."

She instructed Pepper to jiggle her line up and down so the cod at the bottom would think the bait was alive. The line was wrapped around a piece of wood wedged at both ends, and it extended down through the water until it disappeared in the shadowy depths. She jiggled the line and waited. The afternoon sun glinted off the water. The boat rocked gently in the lapping waves, almost lulling her to sleep.

Then she felt a definite tug. She grabbed the wood tightly and began to wind the line in.

"That's it," Grandma encouraged her. "Is it struggling?"

"It feels heavy," said Pepper, imagining a gigantic fish at the other end. "It's pulling good and steady."

"Might be kelp."

And sure enough, a tangle of kelp seaweed eventually surfaced.

"That's the trouble with jigging for cod," said Grandma as she helped free the hook. "They like to hide down there deep in the kelp, and you're as likely to snag some of that as you are to catch a fish. Try again. You'll get something soon enough."

Pepper leaned over the edge of the boat and turned the piece of wood end over end, letting the line unwind again. The lead weights above the hook dragged the line downwards. Pepper jiggled it up and down. A summer breeze teased her hair. The boat floated lazily in the current. The sun crept farther across the wide blue sky. Once in a while Grandma would pull on the oars to reposition the boat.

Pepper laid her head on her arm and looked towards Middle Island. Ray's shack wasn't visible—it faced the open ocean on the other side. But she recognized Starshine in a long skirt dancing along a beached log. Huckle was playing a harmonica. Pepper could hear snatches of his music across the water. Grandma waved and they waved back.

"Starshine! Huckle! Can you come for supper tonight?" yelled Grandma.

"What time?" Starshine called.

"About six thirty."

"Groovy! See you then."

Grandma turned to Pepper. "I'm so glad I met those two. They've got a fresh approach to life. Interesting ideas. It makes you look at things a little differently. Not only that, they're lovely people, both of them. I enjoy their company, and I think it's good for them too. You know when they moved up here to Canada, they had to leave all their friends and family behind. It must be lonely for them." Then she added, "Now we better catch a fish, or I don't know what we're going to feed them."

Pepper jiggled her line and waited for something to happen. Over towards the point, April's house was partially visible through the trees. Two people were walking on the beach below. She could see their silhouettes as they rounded the point. One had long hair; it must be April. The other was a young man. Pepper squinted against the sun, trying to see. Was it Everett? No, the build did not look like Everett's. It was someone more muscular. The way he walked, almost with a swagger, looked familiar. Pepper sat up and shielded her eyes. Ray? It couldn't be. That would be impossible. Ray was in hiding.

Just then there was a twitch on the end of her fishing line.

"I got a nibble," she called out excitedly. The nibble turned into a sharp tug that almost pulled the piece of wood out of her hand. She grabbed on tightly. Something was pulling and fighting on the other end. "It's a real fish this time. I can feel it struggling," she yelled.

"Hold firm. Every time it relaxes for a second, pull it in a bit more."

Pepper wound up the line, little by little. Suddenly something came splashing to the surface. It was brown and orange and slippery. It seemed to be all head and no body. Huge, bulging eyes stared at her, a fearsome creature.

"It's a nice one," yelled Grandma, reaching for the net.

"A nice one! Are you sure?" Pepper thought she had never seen an uglier fish.

"Of course I'm sure. It's a nice big cod!" Grandma said, scooping up the fish and depositing it into the boat. It flip-flopped, gasping and wide-eyed, at their feet.

Pepper let out a shriek and jumped up.

"Sit down," ordered Grandma. "You're rocking the boat. You'll tip us into the water."

Pepper sat down and pulled her feet up out of the way. Grandma grabbed the wooden bat from under her seat and smacked the fish over the head a couple of times. Each time she did, Pepper let out another shriek. Finally the fish lay still.

"We'll eat well tonight," said Grandma.

Pepper stared doubtfully at the slippery creature with its thick lips and coarse scales. She could not imagine touching such a thing, let alone eating it.

That evening at supper Pepper made herself try a small bite of fish. It was coated in crispy cracker crumbs, fried in butter, and drizzled with tangy lemon juice. Pepper savoured the taste on her tongue. Fish had never tasted as good.

As she ate, her daring secret idea resurfaced, as it had many times over the past few days. She'd tried to keep it buried away, but it would not stay there. It had evolved from its slim beginnings into a fully formed plan that kept percolating in her head. When the plan had first struck her, it had seemed too outrageous to even consider. It was dangerous. It was risky. The thought of it gave her a prickly feeling of pins and needles. But she knew she didn't want to let the chance slip away. She looked from Grandma to Everett, both intent on their fish. Wouldn't they be surprised to know what she was thinking right now.

Starshine and Huckle were crowded in at the kitchen table too. "This fish is far out, man," exclaimed Huckle. He was wearing a sheepskin vest and bell-bottomed pants with patches. His beard was sandy coloured and his long hair was tied back in a ponytail. A ponytail on a man! Pepper could imagine what Chloe's mom would say about that.

Pepper swallowed another bite and then said proudly, "It's the first fish I ever caught."

Starshine licked the last of her fish off her fork. "Cool!"

She was wearing a tie-dyed cotton skirt that went all the way down to her ankles.

"Yeah, groovy!" agreed Huckle. "You can invite us for supper anytime you catch a fish."

After the dishes had been washed, they sat out on the porch, and Huckle and Starshine talked about their plans for the fall. They wanted to rent a place in town with a couple of friends. Huckle was going to try his hand at building furniture. Starshine was going to set up a loom and start weaving again. She thought she'd be able to sell her blankets at an Arts Co-op store she knew about.

"You should put some of your paintings in the store too," Starshine said to Grandma. "I'll take you there one day. You'll really dig it. It's a happening place."

"That sounds wonderful," said Grandma. Her eyes sparkled at the thought.

Pepper had never met anyone like Huckle and Starshine. Sure, she'd seen hippies back home. She'd been intrigued by their crazy-looking clothes and the slang they used. They didn't seem to have regular jobs or live regular lives like her parents, or her friend's parents. But she'd never said more than a few words to a hippie before, never gotten to know one. Now, as the evening progressed, she found herself liking this odd-looking couple more and more. When the sun started to sink lower in the sky, they thanked Grandma and said goodbye. It was time for them to row back to Middle Island before it got dark.

"I'll help you carry the boat down," offered Pepper. She had been waiting for this moment.

When they got to the water, Pepper made sure no one else was around and then asked, "Huckle, you're a draft dodger, right?"

"You could call me that. Or draft resister. I'm not going to fight in the war. That's why I moved to Canada."

"Have you ever heard about a group in Vancouver who helps draft dodgers? I mean with all the paperwork and the laws here in Canada? So they don't get sent back to the States again and end up in the army after all ... or even go to jail?"

"Yeah. It's called the Vancouver Committee to Aid American War Objectors. We talked to them when we came across the border and they helped us out with our immigration papers."

Starshine piped in. "There are two main guys who work there. Both of them are named Peter. The two Peters, that's what we always call them."

"How would somebody find them in Vancouver?"

"There's a place downtown on West Hastings Street right across from a big department store, Woodward's," said Huckle. "The store has a giant *W* sign on top of the building. Everyone knows the *W*. It's a landmark. So it's right across the street. You go up about six flights of stairs and that's where the committee has an office. That's where the two Peters work. People go and hang out there. People like us, Americans who have moved here because of the war." He paused. "What do you want to know for?"

Pepper had already prepared her answer. "I met someone who could use their help. He was in the army and he got in trouble and he ran away."

"I see. A deserter," Huckle said. "People are harder on deserters than they are on draft resistors. I could talk to him if you want."

Pepper grinned. Things were turning out exactly the way she'd hoped. "Would you? Thanks, Huckle. I'll ask him."

The next day Pepper found Ray sitting in the sun at the front door of his shack, strumming his guitar. "Hey, long time, no see," he greeted her.

"I came by the day before yesterday. I knocked. Where were you?"

"I must have been sleeping. Sorry. I didn't hear you."

"Sleeping in the middle of the day?"

"A siesta." He paused. "Why didn't you come yesterday?"

"I couldn't. My grandma wanted to take me fishing. Here you go." Pepper set a brown paper bag down on the step. "I brought you some more food."

"Thanks. Well, I'm glad you're here now." A warm smile lit up his face. "There's something I want you to listen to."

"What is it?"

Ray picked up his guitar and played a few chords. "It's a song I'm working on. It's not finished yet. I've just got two verses so far." He began with a simple melody on the strings, then started to sing.

Once a young girl appeared before me
Wrapped in the tissue of a dream
And when I awoke, she was still there
As real as any girl I'd ever seen

She had hair as red as sunsets
She had freckles on her nose
Her smile bloomed oh so sweetly
Just like a summer rose

Pepper blinked hard, trying to hold back the tears. She'd never had a song written for her before.

"Do you like it?"

"I love it."

"I'm glad," Ray said as he put down his guitar. His expression changed. "Have you heard anything from Ajax?"

"No," Pepper said reluctantly. "I went into town a few days ago. I called his mother, but she hasn't talked to him."

Ray sighed heavily and put his face in his hands.

"But I think I found someone else who can help you," Pepper added quickly.

Ray lifted his head. "Really?"

"Huckle. He came to Canada because he didn't want to be drafted, and guess what? He knows all about that group in Vancouver."

"Whoa!" said Ray, putting up his hand. "Slow down. You told some guy called Huckle about me?"

"Not exactly. I didn't tell him your name or where you're hiding. He's met the people in that group and they helped him. He understands what it's like."

Ray looked uncertain. "I don't want anyone else to know where I am, though ..."

"Okay. I'll tell you what. Huckle lives in one of the shacks on the other side of the island, just over the bluff. We can climb up there and find a good spot where we can see everything. When the coast is clear, I'll go down and get him and bring him to you. That way he won't have to know where you're staying."

Pepper could see that Ray was nervous, but finally he said, "All right. I'll do it."

"There's one other thing," Pepper added quietly. She knew he wouldn't like what she had to say next. "I also told Huckle's girlfriend, Starshine, about you."

"Pepper!" Ray blurted out. Then he rolled his eyes. "Anyone else?"

"No. That's it." Pepper paused. "Do you still want to go through with it?"

Ray took in a long, slow breath and blew it out again. He looked at Pepper and nodded his head.

When they'd found a remote spot on the bluff where Ray could hide, Pepper climbed down to Huckle and Starshine's shack. She knocked on the door, but there was no answer. The wind chimes tinkled softly. The prayer flags draped over the railing waved gently in the breeze. She knocked again, louder this time, but there was still no response.

Then Bus came walking along the beach. "Huckle and Starshine are gone. They said they were going to a big concert somewhere outside Vancouver," he called out to her.

"Vancouver! But I just saw them last night. They didn't say anything about that."

"They just decided to go this morning. A spur-of-the-moment thing."

"How long are they going to be gone?"

"I don't know. It's an open-air event in a farmer's field, they said. Vancouver Pop Festival. It goes on for days. Lots of bands. Everyone camps out."

"Thanks," said Pepper. But under her breath she groaned.

CHAPTER 16

The Escape Plan

When she told Ray that Huckle and Starshine were gone, Pepper could see the disappointment on his face. They both sat dejected. Neither of them felt like talking.

"If we'd known they were going over to Vancouver today," Pepper finally said, "you might have been able to go with them. Now we can't even talk to them, let alone ask them to help you."

"It's like bad luck follows me everywhere. What else can possibly go wrong?"

At that moment Pepper glanced towards Ghost Island and was startled to see two blue-uniformed policemen. "Quick. Get down," she hissed.

Moving fast, Pepper and Ray dropped down behind a rocky outcropping.

"What do you think they're doing over there?" Pepper said. Her heart was thumping hard in her chest.

"I bet they're looking for me."

"But what would tip them off now, after all this time?"

"The people over on Ghost Island. They would have seen the broken window. They would have known someone's been there."

They watched as the policemen talked to the owners of the shack and looked around. After some time the officers returned to the beach and started walking over to Middle Island, straight towards Pepper and Ray. They crouched down a little more, and Pepper could feel herself trembling. Several minutes later they heard knocking on the door of the shack directly below them.

"They're at Huckle and Starshine's shack!" whispered Pepper.

"Shhh."

"What do you think they want with Huckle and Starshine?"

"Maybe they heard they'd come here to escape the draft. Maybe they want to see their immigration papers."

After several minutes had passed, the policemen walked away. Pepper was relieved—until she realized they were headed towards Ray's shack on the other side of the island. Ray and Pepper crawled back along the rocks to get a better view.

"They're at the crevice in the rock," whispered Pepper. "Did you lock the door?"

Ray pulled a key from his pocket and dangled it. "There was an extra key in the kitchen drawer. I found it the first day."

"They're going to see the broken window."

"Nope," Ray shook his head. "I cleared the glass away, and I stuck the covering back on again. It'll just look like an empty shack."

They waited. Pepper's legs shook. She didn't want Ray to think she was a scaredy-cat, though, so she steadied herself and put on a brave face. Finally the police squeezed back through the crevice and headed to the car park. The tide was starting to come in.

"If they'd come a few minutes earlier, they would have found you there," said Pepper. "That's one thing that went right today."

Ray smiled ruefully, and then his expression became serious. "Pepper, I can't stay here anymore. It's too risky."

Pepper felt her stomach drop. "Don't go yet. Please."

"I don't want to leave, Pepper, but I have to."

"But what will you do? Where will you go?"

"I don't know yet."

"Can't you stay just a little bit longer? Because I've been thinking about a plan that might work."

"You have? What is it?"

"Well, I haven't quite worked all the details out." Pepper wanted to stall Ray as long as possible, and she glanced towards the main island. "I better go now. The tide has turned, but I'll come back tomorrow. I'll tell you my idea then."

"Okay," Ray said after a pause. "But I'm serious. I need to leave very soon."

"Did you hear the police were over here this afternoon?" said Chloe's mom later that day. She was peeling potatoes for supper.

"Really?" said Pepper and Chloe at the same time. They tried to keep their expressions innocent. Pepper had already filled Chloe in on the events of the day: how she and Ray had just missed seeing Huckle, and how the police had come snooping around Ray's cabin. She hadn't said anything about her plan, though. She kept that to herself. The last thing she wanted was someone trying to talk her out of it.

"Oh, yes," Chloe's mom continued. "I'm surprised you didn't see them. They must have been over every square inch of the place. They were asking if anyone had noticed anything out of the ordinary. I bet they were checking up on those hippies over on Middle Island, though they didn't come right out and say it."

"Why would they want to check up on the hippies?" asked Chloe.

"To make sure everything is above board. Who knows what those hippies get up to? Have you seen that young man with the long hair? I thought he was a girl the first time I saw him."

"Having long hair isn't exactly a crime, Mom."

"No. But they might be up to other things. You never know."

"Like what?"

"Drugs. Devil worship. Could be anything. You never know with those draft dodgers. They sneak across the border, bringing all their revolutionary ideas with them, and they think they can just live here amongst good law-abiding people and no one's going to bat an eye. Well, anyone with an ounce of common sense can see they're nothing but trouble."

"Is it against the law for them to live here?"

"Well, no. But you just have to take one look at them with their love beads and peace signs and such. They could stand some watching, that's all I'm saying." She shook her head. "The police were interested in that shack on Ghost Island too. They wanted to know if anyone had noticed anything unusual going on over there."

"Why?"

"They said there'd been a break-in. It looked like someone had been living there for a while. A squatter."

"Do they know who it was?"

Chloe's mom picked up another potato and scraped away, the skin peeling off in brown swaths until a glistening white version emerged. "Some no-good layabout, I'd bet. Could be a bunch of them. Probably friends of those hippies on Middle Island. That would be my guess." She poked the eye from the potato with the tip of the scraper, checked it over, and put it with the rest.

A few hours later Pepper sat deep in thought on the Periwinkle's front porch. Grandma was bent over one of her canvases, daubing on paint.

"You're quiet tonight," said Grandma.

"I'm just thinking."

"Did you hear the police came over to the island today?"

"Oh? What did they want?"

"I'm sure it wouldn't be anything serious. Probably just wanted to talk to someone. It's so hard to get hold of people here. No phones. No mail. You know what it's like."

"Grandma?"

"Yes?"

"Nothing."

Grandma eyed her painting critically. "Do you think there's too much green in this?"

It was a painting of an arbutus tree with tangled roots clutching the edge of a rocky cliff.

"I think it looks good."

"Mmm. Maybe a bit too much green." And she took her brush and stroked on some reddish-brown paint.

When Pepper woke up the next morning, she knew what she had to do. She tugged the envelope with her bus money out from behind the apple crate and stuffed it in her pocket. Then she waited until the afternoon, when the tide had gone out far enough, before setting off for Middle Island. She cast a worried eye upwards. The sky was iron grey, and there was a prickly tension in the air. It felt as if the whole world was holding its breath.

Pepper rushed up the stairs and banged on the door. As soon as Ray opened it, she blurted, "Here's my plan. We don't need Huckle to help us. He did tell me some stuff. And we can figure out the rest ourselves."

"What did he tell you?"

"The group in Vancouver is called the Committee to Aid American War Objectors. There are two guys called Peter. The two Peters. They have an office downtown, right across the street from Woodward's. That's a store with a great big *W* on top. Huckle said you can't miss it. Hastings Street, I think he said. You go up six flights of stairs and there's the office. That's where all the draft dodgers go. The deserters too."

"Wow. You did really well, Pepper." As Ray looked at her, she felt a glow of pride.

"But wait. That's only the first part of my plan. I'm coming to the best part," Pepper went on eagerly. "We can go together. I've got it all figured out. After the committee helps you get everything straightened out, we can go down to California and find our mom."

Ray shifted uncomfortably. "You can't be serious. There's no way you're going with me. It's dangerous. The police are looking for me. Besides, I don't have any money. I'll have to hitchhike."

"She's my mom too," said Pepper stubbornly. "And I can help along the way. I can do the talking so people won't notice you so much. Besides ..." Pepper pulled out the envelope and shook it in front of him. "I've got money."

Ray took the envelope and counted the bills. "Where'd you get all this?"

"It's supposed to be for the bus ride home."

"Look, Pepper. You have to use this to go back home. You've got a home. You've got a family already. That's where you belong."

"No! They're not my real parents. It's not the same. I don't want to go back. I want to go with you."

"But your family will be worried out of their minds. Think about that."

"I've already thought about it. I can't tell them because they wouldn't let me go. So I'll do it and tell them later. I've got it all worked out," Pepper said before he could protest any further. "We've got enough money to get us started. We can pick a night, and when the tide's out we'll walk over to the car park. Grandma keeps her car key on top of the visor. We can borrow her car and drive to the ferry. You know how to drive, right?"

Ray nodded.

"Okay. We'll leave the car at the ferry and catch the first boat in the morning to Vancouver. We'll get on a bus on the other side. It's that simple."

Ray didn't say anything.

"Well, how about it?" prompted Pepper.

"I don't know," said Ray, shaking his head. "If you go missing, there're going to be even more police out looking."

"No, no. I've thought of that too. I'll leave a note saying

that I've gone over to Chloe's for the day, and I'm going to sleep over. By the time they start looking for me, we'll be long gone."

"What about stealing your grandma's car?"

"We'll just borrow it to get to the ferry. She won't even notice it's gone if we time it right. She only uses it once in a while."

Still, Ray looked unconvinced.

"She's going into town tomorrow," Pepper pressed on. "So we could even do it tomorrow night."

"Let me think about it."

"What's there to think about?"

"I've got to think what's best for you."

"This is what's best for me. Finding my real mom," Pepper insisted.

"Even after I meet the two Peters, and they help me with my paperwork, I might not be able to cross the border again. Ever. You know that, don't you? I might not be able to go to California and look for our mom."

"It'll work. It has to. We have to try at least. Look. You hold on to the money. We'll plan for tomorrow night. Deal?" She stuck out her hand.

Ray paused for a moment. Then he took her hand and shook it. "Deal."

"What time should we meet up?"

"I've been keeping track of the tides. It'll be very early in the morning, about four o'clock, before the tide is out far enough. We can walk over to the car park separately. I'll meet you there."

"Do you have a flashlight? It will be hard to get over these rocks in the dark."

"There's one here, but I'm not going to use it. I don't

want to draw attention to myself. Besides, there'll be the light of the moon." Ray fell quiet. Then he reached over and smoothed one of her unruly curls back off her forehead. He had an expression Pepper couldn't quite read. Was he going to say how much he appreciated her help? That he liked having her as a sister? That he was glad they had found each other? But then the look vanished. The moment passed.

"You better be getting back" was all he said.

"Tomorrow night, right?"

"Right. Four in the morning at the car park."

"You won't sleep through?"

"No. I doubt I'll sleep at all that night."

"Me too. I'll be too excited." But even as she spoke, Pepper began to wonder if she might, indeed, fall asleep. It was one thing to stay awake until midnight, but quite another thing to wait until four in the morning. Could she borrow her grandma's alarm clock? No! It would wake everyone else up too. She'd have to figure something out, but for now she didn't want Ray to sense her uncertainty. "You can count on me!" she said.

A few minutes later, as she squeezed through the crevice, Ray caught up with her. "I almost forgot. I made this for you," he said, and he pressed an object into her hand.

It was a carved fish made from a piece of cedar, every detail perfect, right down to the scales and fins. Pepper turned it over, admiring it from every angle. It was even better than the bird carving she'd wanted. She didn't know what to say. When she looked up, he was already halfway back to the shack.

"Thank you," she called after him. But she wasn't sure he heard.

CHAPTER 17

A Summer Storm

Pepper's eyes flew open. The vividness of her dream had jolted her awake. Outside the wind was howling around the shack. Rain dashed against the window. Her dream had been full of wind and rain too. There had been a boat at night. She'd been struggling to pull the oars, trying to get to shore. The oars kept slipping from her hands. They were the wrong oars, she realized, much too small for the boat, so short they barely reached the water. When she did manage to get the oar blades into the water, they softened like limp spaghetti. She couldn't make any headway. She was fighting the wind. Waves were crashing over the sides. She was soaking wet. Chilled to the bone.

Pepper sat straight up in bed. Her heart was thumping hard. She tried to think calmly. *It's not tonight*, she told herself. *It's tomorrow night we're supposed to meet.*

But her heart kept hammering. She could not quiet her fears. He was going. She was sure of it. He was going tonight. And he was going without her.

Pepper threw the covers aside and swung her legs out of bed. She dragged a sweater on over her pajamas, pulled on a pair of pants, and pushed her feet into her runners. At Everett's curtain she paused. Should she wake him up?

But what if the same thing happened as last time? She'd made Everett come with her after one of her dreams, and they'd ended up being stranded on Ghost Island. She'd been wrong then. Maybe she was wrong again.

No, she decided. She was going to do this alone. She tiptoed by the curtain, took the flashlight, and let herself out the door.

As soon as she stepped outside, the wind caught her hair and whipped it around her head. The rain pelted down, shockingly cold. The moon, covered in clouds, cast no light at all. It was so dark she couldn't even see her feet on the stairs. There was a low rumbling sound. What was that? Thunder?

She turned on the flashlight and stumbled down to the beach. The tide was up. It was a bad time to cross over to the car park. But she had to get there somehow. If she didn't hurry she'd miss him. She'd have to take Grandma's old wooden rowboat. She dashed back and found it in the grass above the high-tide mark. It was upside down. She tried with all her might to turn it over, but she could only lift it partway up. She couldn't flip it. It was just too heavy.

Another low rumble. Louder this time. Definitely thunder.

She should go back in, Pepper thought. Get out of the storm. But then she had another idea. Chloe's family had a yellow rubber dinghy. Not only would it be lighter, but it was on the side of Shack Island closest to the car park. She wouldn't have to row as far. And that was a good thing, Pepper told herself, considering she wasn't the greatest rower in the world. She scrambled up the path, past the fort, up to the top where the wind howled through the trees, and down the other side.

All the shacks were in darkness. The yellow dinghy was stashed under Chloe's veranda. She pulled it out. It was light and the wind buffeted it, so she had to hold it tight. Two plastic oars and a life jacket were lashed inside. She dragged it down the rocky beach to the water's edge, jumped in, put on the life jacket, and untied the oars. The boat rocked in the waves. The current was strong. It was hard to make the dinghy go in the right direction. She pulled on the oars, straining with her whole body. It was impossible to see in the darkness, but she had an uneasy sense the boat was drifting farther from the car park.

A flash of lightning arced across the sky. For a split second everything was illuminated. She saw then that, just as she feared, she was being swept in the wrong direction.

A sick, panicky feeling formed in the pit of Pepper's stomach. She'd never rowed a boat by herself before, let alone in the middle of a storm, and at night. She pulled harder on the oars. The rain soaked right through to her skin. Her muscles ached. Her hands were getting rubbed raw. Finally she reached the other side, a good distance from the car park, but at least she had made it. She hauled the dinghy high up on the bank, tied it to a tree, and hiked back along the storm-lashed shoreline towards the car park.

It looked deserted. She could see only the dark outlines of the trees and the cars. As she got closer, she could make out Grandma's Rambler, nosed up to the salal bushes. She shone her light inside. It was empty. She opened the door and crawled into the back seat, out of the wind and rain.

Ray wasn't there after all. What had she been thinking? Ray wouldn't leave without her. He'd promised. Not only was it the wrong night, it was the wrong time of night. He'd have had to find a boat to get across, just like she had. In the middle of a storm, too. No, Pepper decided, it didn't make sense. At that very moment he was probably asleep, warm and dry, in his shack over on Middle Island.

She should never have come out in a storm, all alone, just because of a dream. She should have known better. If she'd only stopped a minute to reason it out, she'd be asleep, safe and sound, in her bed right now too.

Pepper shivered. She was ice cold and dripping wet. She'd just take a moment to warm up, she thought, and then she'd row back again, before anyone found she was missing. She hated the thought of going out into the storm again. She couldn't even see through the window. It was too dark, and the glass was awash with rain.

Suddenly the car door burst open. There was a rush of wind and rain. Something large and bulky was being shoved into the back seat. Pepper scooted quickly out of the way, down onto the floor, hoping she wouldn't be discovered in the shadows. The door slammed shut and then the front door opened. Pepper hazarded a furtive peek over the back seat and saw Ray climbing into the car. He was wet right through. He tossed his duffel bag onto the passenger seat and ran a hand back through his hair, pushing the rain off his face and head. He shook his head like a dog. Then he felt along the top of the sun visor, pulled out the key, and started the engine.

Pepper was too shocked to say anything. She crouched back down again and felt along the hard object that had been shoved into the back seat. His guitar case. Of course.

The headlights shone through a torrent of rain. The windshield wipers flicked back and forth. Ray put the car into reverse. His eyes glanced up into the rear-view mirror. Quickly, Pepper ducked down even lower. She held her breath, waiting. Fortunately, he didn't see her; he was too intent on checking the area behind the car. She felt the car back out of the parking space, a pause, and then it moved forward over the bumpy road. The ride became smoother when they turned from the gravel road onto the asphalt.

Pepper's shock changed to fury. Ray had promised her. And she'd believed him. She could understand why he wanted to leave, with the police sniffing around, but it was a betrayal to go without her. Well, she would show him! She was going to give him a good scare. She'd sit up and tap him on the shoulder.

But just then the car pulled off onto a side road. It went down a short distance and stopped. Pepper was surprised to see the gates to April's house lit up in the headlights. Ray got out of the car without turning the engine off.

Pepper sat up. Why had he stopped here? The headlights shone as Ray ran through the gates and up the driveway in the rain. He stooped to pick up a handful of gravel and circled to the side of the house. One by one he tossed pieces of gravel up against a window. The window opened. Then a moment later the front door opened. April came out. She was wearing a long white nightie. Her hair was loose.

Ray took her up in his arms. He kissed her.

Pepper blinked hard. She could not believe her eyes. She didn't even think April and Ray knew each other. And here they were together right in front of her. Kissing!

A few niggling thoughts floated to the surface of Pepper's memory. Hadn't Ray had a good long look at

April through the binoculars that day with Everett? And what about that time when she was fishing with Grandma? She'd seen someone who looked like Ray walking around the point with April. And the time he hadn't answered the door of the shack? He'd said he'd been having a siesta, but maybe he'd been off seeing April then too.

Ray had been hiding a secret. He'd kept it from her, and he'd kept it from Everett. All this time he'd been coaching Everett on how to approach April, he'd been after her himself. The whole idea disgusted Pepper.

Ray let April go. He bent his head down, said a few words to her, then turned back towards the car. April stood in the rain, watching him.

Suddenly Pepper hated Ray. If he'd been keeping this a secret, what else had he been keeping from her? Maybe he'd been lying about everything! She grabbed the door handle and jumped out. Ray wouldn't be able to see her. The glare from the headlights would be too bright. He might hear the car door close, but she didn't care. She dashed through the rain and down the road, then ducked into the salal bushes.

The car backed out, drove slowly by, and turned onto the main road. As she watched its red tail lights disappear around the corner, she hoped she'd made the right decision. There goes my chance to find my mother, she thought. There goes my brother out of my life.

Pepper didn't know what to do next. Water coursed down her cheeks, a mixture of rain and tears. Ray had stolen her money. He'd stolen Grandma's car. He'd stolen the girl Everett liked. And he'd left without her. He hadn't even bothered to say goodbye. That was the thing that stung most of all.

She made herself push against the gusting wind, back down the road towards the car park. It was pitch black, and, too late, she realized she'd left the flashlight in the car. She stumbled along the beach until she found the little rubber boat still tied up to the tree. She felt around in the darkness and located the oars, but she couldn't find the life jacket.

The wind had gained strength. Waves were smashing against the shore. Pepper struggled to get the boat in the water. She dragged herself in and pulled on the oars. The boat tossed from side to side in the waves. A whoosh of water cascaded in. Pepper's feet were ankle deep in the brine. The wind was pushing the boat in the wrong direction. Pepper pulled harder. A wave caught one of the oars and yanked it out of her hands. The oar washed away out of reach. Another wave struck the boat broadside. The boat listed to the side. It was about to tip. Pepper hung on tightly.

"Help!" she called out. "Help me!"

But she was too far from the shore for anyone to hear her.

CHAPTER 18

Nothing but Lies

The little boat lurched, then righted itself. But water kept pouring in. Pepper clung to the boat. Her hands were so cold she knew she wouldn't be able to hold on much longer. If she let go, she would slip into the water.

If only she hadn't lost her other oar. If only she had the life jacket. If only she was closer to shore.

But none of that was the case, and Pepper came to a terrible realization. On this stormy night, all alone, she was going to drown.

"Hold on!" A voice out of the blackness.

Pepper looked around but could not see anyone. Was she hallucinating?

But the voice came again. "Hold on, Pepper. I'm coming."

She knew that voice. It was Everett's. A moment later he appeared out of the night. He was rowing Grandma's old wooden rowboat. It was sturdier in the waves than the flimsy rubber boat she was clutching. He pulled alongside. Pepper reached over and hung on to the edge. Everett grabbed her arms and dragged her up and over. She tumbled into the boat like a waterlogged rag doll.

A fierce gust of wind caught the little yellow rubber dinghy and tossed it away across the bounding waves. A moment later it had vanished into the dark night.

"Here, put this on," yelled Everett, and he flung an orange life jacket in her direction. "And stay down low, out of the wind." He began to heave on the oars.

Pepper pulled the life jacket over her head and tied it tight as she shivered in a wet huddle in the bottom of the boat. She was so cold she thought she might pass out.

"How did you know I was here?" she managed to yell back.

Everett grunted with each stroke. "I heard you go out." Grunt. "I followed you up over the bluff." Grunt. "But I couldn't go as fast as you because you had the flashlight." Grunt. "When I saw you head out in that little dinghy ..." Grunt. "I called out for you to stop, but you didn't hear me." "So I went back and got Grandma's boat." "Took every muscle I had to drag it down to the water." The wind was breaking his words into fragments. "Probably scraped all the paint off the bottom of the boat." "Took forever to get around the bluff." "Fighting the wind the whole way."

Pepper waited. She expected him to ask what she'd been doing. But he didn't. He was concentrating on his rowing.

Finally Pepper said, "Ray left. I saw him go."

Everett nodded. "I thought so."

Pepper figured Everett would be angry with her for being so foolish—coming out in a storm at night, almost drowning—but he didn't say a word. He just kept rowing.

"Thanks for coming out tonight," she yelled, close to tears. "Thanks for saving me."

"That's what a brother does," Everett yelled back. He kept rowing.

Pepper woke up late the next morning. Her first thought was about Everett. He had saved her, even though it meant putting himself in danger.

Not like Ray.

A sharp pain shot through her. Ray was tall and handsome, he told good stories, and, most of all, he was exciting. She used to think all of those things would make a perfect brother. Well, not anymore. She remembered the heartless way Ray had left, without a word, without a thought to her feelings. And she remembered how he had kissed April. The image of the couple in the spotlight of the headlights was burned in her memory. One thing she knew for sure, she was not going to tell Everett about the kiss. It would hurt and humiliate him. She wouldn't tell Chloe, either. Chloe had a thing for Ray. It would hurt her too. She would tell them everything else, but she wouldn't tell them about the kiss.

Pepper sat up, grabbed the carved fish from the apple crate table, and tossed it under the bed. Stupid fish. She couldn't believe she'd ever liked it. Then she pulled the covers over her head and groaned.

"Are you okay?" Grandma said from the other side of the curtain.

"Uh-huh."

"Well, you better get up before the day's half over. Don' forget we're going into town later. I've got a long gr list."

Pepper threw the covers back. She looked out the window at the hard, unforgiving light. The storm had washed everything bare. The sky was clear and intensely bright. Here we go, she thought anxiously. As soon as they got to the car park, Grandma was going to see that the Rambler was gone.

Pepper found some dry clothes to wear and tugged her comb through her tangled hair. When she emerged from her bedroom cubicle, Everett was already at the kitchen table warming his hands on a mug of hot milky tea. He shot her a quick look, one eyebrow raised. Pepper returned the look. It was like passing a secret note back and forth.

That afternoon, when they'd lugged the empty water bottles and laundry bag up the bank at the other side, Grandma scratched her head. "Where's the car?" she said. "I parked it right here, where I always do. At least I think I did." She walked around the maple trees, looking at all the cars. Finally she stopped. It was obvious her car was not there. "Isn't that the strangest thing. What could have happened to it?"

Pepper forced herself to speak up. "Maybe someone stole it."

"Stole it? I can't imagine why they'd want to do that," said Grandma. "Besides, we've never had a problem like that around here before. It's always been perfectly safe."

"Well, the car was unlocked and the key was inside. Anyone could have wandered by and taken it," said Everett.

"That's true," agreed Pepper, grateful for his support.

Grandma put her hands on her hips and surveyed the car park again in disbelief. "Isn't that something? I hate to say it, but maybe you're right."

"What are we going to do now?" asked Pepper.

"Well, I suppose we should report it to the police," Grandma said. She sounded shaken. "We'll have to find a phone."

When Pepper saw how upset Grandma was, she felt a heavy burden of guilt. Maybe she should speak up. Maybe she should admit what had happened last night. But the real story—the storm, Pepper almost drowning, Everett's rescue, the two of them harbouring a fugitive—would upset Grandma even more. No, Pepper decided, it was better to remain quiet.

"We can stash our bottles and laundry here and walk down to the store. There's a pay phone there. And I guess we should pick up a few of the groceries at the same time," Grandma said. They set off down the road.

Half an hour after the phone call was made, a policeman arrived at the store. He was not one of the officers who had searched Shack Island a few days before. This one was middle-aged and had crinkles around his eyes. He drove them back to the car park and walked around, poking in the bushes. He made notes in a notepad. "You can't be too careful these days, ma'am. It's probably not a good idea to leave your key in the car."

"But who could have taken it?" asked Grandma.

The policeman shook his head. "It's hard to say. Might have been anyone. We'll keep our eyes open and let you know if we find it."

"It's always been safe here. I've never locked up my car."

"The world's a different place now, ma'am. Low-lifes. Petty thieves. Drug addicts. Kids wanting to go out for a joyride. You never know."

"My, my, I never thought it would come to this ..."

"Oh, you'd be surprised what goes on."

"But not around here. Surely."

"I'm afraid so, ma'am. I'll give you one example: there's that young juvenile delinquent who escaped from Brannen Lake a while back, not too far from here. We're still looking for him."

Pepper felt her breath catch.

Grandma said, "Oh, yes, I remember reading about him in the paper. What did he do?"

"He's a troublemaker. He's been in and out of jail since grade school. Breaking into people's houses, theft, vandalism, you name it. He's got a list of offences as long as your arm."

The policeman's words swirled around Pepper's head. Once again she found herself wondering if the escaped juvenile delinquent might be Ray. He had denied it when she'd confronted him, but in many ways it seemed more believable than the story he had told her.

Pepper sank down slowly to sit on a log.

"Are you all right, dear?" asked Grandma.

"Just hot. Hot and tired," she said.

"I am too. I think we all are. Let's go home now. We can think about going into town another day."

As they carried their bottles and laundry back to the island, Pepper lagged behind. She could not stop thinking about how Ray had betrayed her. Everything he'd said about being a deserter and trying to locate the group in Vancouver might have been a lie, an elaborate ruse to throw her off track.

And who knew what else he'd lied about. Maybe he wasn't even her brother! Had he just pretended to be so that she'd help him hide out and then escape? She tried to recall the conversation at the beginning of the summer when they'd concluded they were brother and sister. She went over and over it. How much had she given away? How much could he simply have guessed?

As Pepper turned this idea over in her mind she became more and more certain. Ray wasn't her brother after all. She'd been tricked. How easily she'd been taken in! She should have doubted a brother and sister would ever find each other in such a way. It was too far-fetched. Why had she not realized that before? She could imagine what Ray had thought when he'd met her. He would have seen a silly girl who desperately wanted to find her real family. He had taken advantage of that.

And what about the bus money he'd stolen? What was she going to do when it came time to go home? This new worry made Pepper feel so queasy she thought she might throw up, but Grandma and Everett had stopped and were waiting for her to catch up. She swallowed hard and made her feet keep moving.

As they passed Chloe's shack, Chloe came out onto the veranda and waved to them. "Our little dinghy's missing. We've looked all over. Have you seen it?"

"Your dinghy? No, we haven't," said Grandma.

Everett and Pepper both shook their heads, trying to look innocent.

"We had it stored under the veranda right here." She came down the stairs and pointed to where it used to be. "I know it was stormy last night, but I didn't think it would blow away. Mr. English over on Middle Island thought he lost his boat too, but he found it on the other side today, not far from the car park."

Pepper had a very good idea how Mr. English's boat had ended up there, but she was careful not to let on. Grandma, meanwhile, was saying, "Well, it certainly was quite a storm. All these boats going missing. And to top it off, my car's gone too."

Chloe's eyes widened. "Gone? You mean … stolen?"

"I'm afraid so."

Chloe turned and yelled at the top of her lungs, "MOM!"

Chloe's mom came to the door. "What?"

"Pepper's grandma's car was stolen!"

"Stolen!" Chloe's mom clapped a hand to her mouth. Then she hurried down the stairs to hear the rest of the story.

Grandma related how the car had gone missing and what the policeman had said.

"I'd bet you anything this all has something to do with those hippies over on Middle Island," said Chloe's mom as she popped a mint in her mouth and chewed on it.

"Why on earth would they have anything to do with it?" Grandma said.

"You just have to take one look at them and you know they're trouble."

"Starshine and Huckle?"

"Is that what they call themselves?"

"I rather like their names. Suits them, don't you think?"

"I don't know. I've never talked to them."

"Well, you should get to know them. Delightful people. Free spirits. They stand up for what they believe in. You have to admire them for that."

Chloe's mom almost choked on her mint.

Pepper caught Chloe's eye and tilted her head to one side. She did the same with Everett. The three of them moved away from the others and Pepper whispered, "He's gone."

"Who's gone?" Chloe said. She wore a blank expression.

"Ray. He left last night. In the storm."

"What? Where did he go?"

"I don't know. I just know he's gone."

Chloe looked crestfallen. "But he didn't say goodbye …"

Pepper pressed her lips together. She glanced over towards Grandma and Chloe's mother. They were still talking. She leaned in closer. "He took Grandma's car."

Chloe stared, her mouth gaping open.

"And you know what?" Pepper went on. "I'm pretty sure Ray wasn't my real brother. He was lying. He lied about that, and he lied about practically everything so we'd help him."

Chloe stared at her. "You're kidding me, right?"

"No, I'm not."

"But he looks like you. Red hair. Freckles. He had me fooled."

"Not me," Everett whispered. "It was too improbable."

Pepper shot Everett a look. "Come on, Everett. He had you fooled too. Admit it."

Everett shook his head firmly. "Not for a second."

Pepper decided to ignore him. She turned back to Chloe. "I bet he wasn't a military deserter after all. He might be that escaped juvenile delinquent from Brannen Lake."

"No!"

"Yes!"

"What do you think, Everett?" asked Chloe.

"Pepper might be right."

Pepper paused to appreciate the moment. It wasn't often that Everett said she was right about something. Then she rushed on to explain what had happened the previous night: how she'd borrowed Chloe's family's dinghy, how Everett had rescued her, and how the dinghy had blown away. She told the entire story, everything except the kiss.

Chloe listened in amazement. "I can't believe you took our dinghy and then lost it! If my mom hears about this, she's going to be madder than a wet hen. I can tell you that."

"I'm sorry, Chloe. I really am. Please don't tell your mom."

"Okay," said Chloe. "But let's all make a promise. None of us will breathe a word about this to anyone else."

Pepper and Everett both solemnly nodded.

Chloe went on. "You could have drowned last night, Pepper, if it wasn't for you, Everett."

"It's scary to think what might have happened," agreed Everett. "I could have easily slept through the whole thing."

"I sure am lucky. I know that," said Pepper. She was going to say lucky to be alive *and* lucky to have a brother like Everett, but she didn't want to embarrass him. Plus, it might go to his head.

Then Grandma called over, "Pepper. Everett. We'd better get going."

As they walked home along the beach, they found one of the dinghy's oars washed up on the shore.

"We can take the bus into town," said Grandma the next day, adjusting her reading glasses and peering at the bus schedule. "We'll carry the empty water bottles and the laundry bag back again. The bus stop is down the road a ways. We've got to get groceries too, so there will be even more to carry on the way home." She picked up her grocery list and put it in her pocket.

Not only that, thought Pepper, but the water bottles would be full and much heavier on the way back. She wasn't looking forward to the trip at all.

They had to take a couple of rest breaks along the way, stopping to put down their loads and rub their hands. Finally they reached the bus stop. Pepper was hot and sweaty. A fly kept buzzing around her head.

"What time is the bus supposed to come?" asked Pepper.

Grandma checked her watch. "Five minutes." She wiped her brow. "Goodness, it's hot! Let's wait off the road, back in the trees where it's cooler."

Pepper was tempted to wait in the shade with Everett and Grandma, but one thing stopped her. She couldn't get the thought of cougars out of her head. Even if there was just one cougar in the forest, Pepper could predict what would happen. The cougar would spot her immediately, pounce on her, and gobble her up. One, two, three, just like that.

"I'll stay here," she insisted. "That way the bus driver will see someone's waiting. It won't go by us." The hot sun made her grumpy, but it felt strangely satisfying to suffer in the heat, a kind of punishment. She deserved it, she told herself, for everything she'd messed up this summer.

Five minutes came and went. "The bus must be late," said Grandma from her cool retreat. "By the way, does either of you know where the flashlight is? I couldn't find it last night."

Everett shook his head. Pepper shrugged. She was getting pretty good at feigning innocence. Probably from all the practice she'd had this summer. And the thought of that made her feel even guiltier.

Another five minutes went by.

"Do you think we missed it?" asked Pepper. The sun was beating down. She could feel sweat trickling down her back.

"Well, if we did, there should be another one in an hour."

"An hour! I'll be fried as crisp as bacon in an hour." That's it, she decided. She'd suffered enough. She'd done her penance. She was going into the woods to wait. So what if a cougar showed up? She'd scare it off, that's what she would do. After everything she'd been through—fighting a storm, almost drowning—scaring away a big cat would be a piece of cake.

Just then a shiny silver car pulled up. April's dad rolled down the window. "I'm heading in to the office. Do you need a ride to town?"

Pepper was glad they weren't going to have to wait another hour. But she wondered what Mr. Ferguson must think of such a ragtag bunch, looking like vagabonds with their meagre belongings.

"That would be lovely," said Grandma. "If it's not out of your way."

"No trouble at all," he said and helped them load up the trunk.

Grandma got in the front seat, and Everett and Pepper climbed in the back. Pepper ran her hand over the leather seats as she sank back into the comfortable cushions. The car was new and luxurious. It even smelled new. Not only that, it was deliciously cool.

"Your car must be air-conditioned," said Everett, looking impressed. Neither Grandma's Rambler nor their dad's station wagon had air conditioning.

Mr. Ferguson glanced at them in the rear-view mirror. "Is it too cold for you?"

"Oh, no! It's perfect," said Pepper. She closed her eyes for a moment and remembered the time when she'd thought the Fergusons might be her real family. What an enticing notion that had been. Pepper allowed herself to drift into a pleasing daydream. Would her bedroom be painted yellow or pink? Yellow, she decided. Definitely yellow. She'd have her own record player. And she'd swim in the pool every day. There'd be airplane trips and rides in convertibles, and anything she wanted.

Stop, she told herself firmly. No matter how much she longed for it, the Fergusons were not her real family. In fact, nothing that summer had turned out the way she'd wanted it to. Once Ray came along, everything turned messy.

Pepper opened her eyes and looked out the window. They were on the outskirts of town now, the houses lined up in tidy rows along the sidewalks. Everyone else, it seemed to Pepper, had neat, orderly lives. But not her.

Grandma was telling Mr. Ferguson about her stolen car, and she was still talking about it when they pulled in to the driveway of her house.

"What a shock that must have been for you," Mr. Ferguson said.

"I still can't believe it. And I don't even want to think about everything I'll have to do now. There's contacting the insurance company and then figuring out how to get another car. What a kafuffle!"

Pepper fidgeted in her seat. Ray had caused all this. It was his fault. She wished he'd never come to Shack Island.

"Why don't you phone the insurance people today? Worry about the rest later," Mr. Ferguson suggested. "I'll tell you what ... how about if I swing by in a couple of hours to take you back? We can make a stop for groceries on the way."

"You're very kind, Michael. Thank you."

Mr. Ferguson waved as he drove off.

Pepper waved back, then turned to Grandma. At first

glance she looked as she always did, dressed in her floppy hat and Bermuda shorts, but there was something different about her appearance now. She seemed smaller and older. More worry lines creased her face.

"Grandma," Pepper said, "maybe your next car can have air conditioning." She felt so bad at that moment she would have given practically anything so that Grandma could have a new car.

The worry lines disappeared and Grandma laughed. "No, no. I don't need anything fancy. Rolling down the windows for fresh air has always worked for me."

When they opened the door to the house, the first thing they did was look through the mail. There was one letter from home, addressed to all three of them. Pepper felt a twinge of disappointment as Grandma read it aloud. At least last time there had been a letter just for her, even if it hadn't been anything special.

" … must be getting very close now. I hope the baby comes early. I feel as big as a house …" Grandma read out. She finished the letter and folded it up. "Isn't it exciting?"

"I can hardly wait," Pepper forced herself to say. What she really thought was that once the baby was born, she might as well lie down, wither up, and be blown off in the wind. No one would notice.

No, that wasn't quite true. Everett would notice. Probably Grandma too.

Pepper squirmed as she wondered what would happen if Grandma found out what Pepper had been up to that summer. Grandma would be shocked and angry, that was a given. But she'd be disappointed in her, as well. That was the part Pepper didn't want to think about.

Later that afternoon, when Mr. Ferguson dropped them

off at the car park, the first thing they saw was the police car. The policeman they'd met the day before was sitting inside. He opened the door when he saw them and stepped out.

"I have some good news for you," he said to Grandma. "We found your car."

Grandma clapped her hands together as a radiant smile bloomed on her face. "You did? Thank goodness! Where was it?"

"At the ferry terminal. It was abandoned there. We think someone's been hiding in one of the shacks. Remember that juvenile delinquent I told you about? It might have been him. We figure he stole your car to get to the ferry. He ditched it there and walked on. He must be somewhere on the mainland now. Maybe even crossed the border into the United States."

"Oh, my!"

"We're checking the car over for evidence, and we'll bring it back in a couple of days. It seems to be in good shape. The key was left on the sun visor."

Pepper and Everett exchanged glances. Neither of them said a word about Ray. They both wanted to forget the whole thing had ever happened.

CHAPTER 19

Blabbermouth

All everyone on Shack Island wanted to talk about for the next few days was the juvenile delinquent who'd escaped from Brannen Lake.

"Imagine," said Chloe's mom to Grandma and Bus, on the beach in front of the Periwinkle. "He was living amongst us all this time, and no one had a clue."

"I should have known something wasn't right," said Bus. "I had a feeling. You know that creepy feeling you get when someone's watching you?"

Chloe's mom nodded her head. "The people over on Ghost Island said he'd been staying in their shack some of the time. He ate all their food. He slept right in their bed!"

Grandma shook her head. "I can't help wondering what kind of sad, unfortunate life that young man must have had. It's such a shame."

Barry Brewster sidled over to Pepper and Everett and

Chloe, who were sitting off to the side. "I know what the three of you have been up to this summer."

Pepper felt her muscles tense. "Don't you have anything better to do than sneak around spying on us all the time?"

"I was not spying."

"You were too. What about that time I found you hiding on the stairs outside our door?"

"I was just trying to hear about the moon landing on the radio."

"Why didn't you listen on your own radio?"

Barry glared back. "Because we don't have one. That's why."

"What do you mean, you don't have one? Everyone has a radio."

"We don't … anymore," he said, quieter now, looking a bit like a deflated balloon. "We used to have a good one, but then my dad hurt his back and now he can't work. He sold some of our stuff so we could pay the rent. We're living out here for the summer 'cause it's cheaper."

Pepper was taken aback. She would never have expected Barry to reveal so much about himself. Maybe she'd been too quick to jump to conclusions about him.

But before Pepper could say anything, Barry puffed himself up again. "I didn't tell you that so you'd feel sorry for me, you know. I don't care what any of you think. I see you guys walking around like you're better than me. Well, here's a news flash. You're not as good as you think you are." He was getting red in the face. "Because I know your little secret."

"We don't have a secret," Pepper said.

A sly smile crossed Barry's face. "Oh, is that right? I've been keeping my eyes and ears open, and you've been helping that guy who escaped from Brannen Lake hide out here."

Pepper felt her anger at Barry boiling up all over again.

But it was Everett who spoke. He looked Barry straight in the eye. "You're just making up stories. Trying to cause problems. You better mind your own business."

Pepper felt a surge of pride. She had never seen Everett stand up to a bully before.

Barry took a step back. He paused for a moment and then turned to Pepper. "You've been taking food to him. You could be in big trouble helping that convict hide out like that."

Before she could stop herself, Pepper blurted out, "We didn't know he was a convict!"

Chloe and Everett groaned.

Barry looked satisfied.

Now that Pepper had said it, there was no going back. "We didn't know he was a criminal," Pepper continued in a low voice. "He told us he'd been in the U.S. army."

"Well, of course he's not going to say he escaped from Brannen Lake."

"I'm just telling you what he told us. He said he'd been in the army. Then he ran away and came to Canada."

Barry smirked. "Do you always believe everything people tell you? Wait until this gets out."

"Don't go being a blabbermouth," warned Pepper.

But it was too late. Barry was already walking over to the group Grandma was talking to. He tapped her on the shoulder. "Have you asked Pepper and Everett what they know about that convict? Chloe too," he said.

The adults looked surprised. "What would they know about him?" Grandma said. "They're as much in the dark as the rest of us."

Barry smiled smugly. "Well, they helped hide him, and they brought him food, and they probably helped him get away."

Grandma gasped.

Bus was the first to speak. "That's gotta be about the craziest thing I've ever heard."

"Chloe, is this true?" Chloe's mom demanded.

"It's not the way it sounds," protested Chloe.

"So, it *is* true! Whatever possessed you to do such a thing? Wait until your father hears about this!" Chloe's mom took Chloe by the arm. "Come along with me, young lady. We're going home right this minute. You're grounded."

There was a long silence after they left. Pepper squirmed uncomfortably. Grandma looked confused and distressed. "Does someone want to explain to me what's going on?" she said.

Pepper took a big breath. "It's my fault," she began. "Don't blame Chloe or Everett. Blame me. I should never have believed Ray. Right from the start, I should never have trusted him."

"Who's Ray?" asked Grandma.

"The escaped convict."

"Why on earth were you helping him hide out on Shack Island?"

"He didn't tell me he was an escaped convict. He said he'd run away from the army in the States. And ..." Pepper stopped. Everyone was waiting for her to continue. Bus and Barry and Grandma were all gaping. "It's not easy talking about this in front of everyone," she finally said.

Grandma sighed deeply and then pointed to a spot farther down the beach. "You and Everett and I will go sit on that log over there and talk about this privately." Once they were out of earshot, Grandma continued, "You've got a lot of explaining to do, Pepper. I expect you to tell me the truth. Do you understand?"

"Yes, ma'am."

Grandma sat down on the log. Pepper and Everett sat next to her. Pepper couldn't think of a time when she'd felt so miserable, weighed down with guilt and regrets. She wished she could crumple up everything that had happened that summer and throw it away like a piece of scrap paper.

"He said he was my brother," she blurted out. "I thought I was helping him."

"Your brother?" repeated Grandma incredulously.

"Yes, from my real family, before I was adopted. He told stories about things that happened years ago … and I believed him."

"You thought some stranger was your brother? Pepper! Honestly! Why didn't you tell me about this?"

"I promised him I wouldn't," Pepper mumbled.

"Pepper! How could you have got yourself into such a situation? An escaped convict—who knows what could have happened? And to think this has been going on and I didn't have an inkling." She shook her head. "I suppose it's because I've been so caught up in my painting."

"It's not your fault, Grandma," Pepper said.

"No. No. I should have been paying more attention." Then Grandma turned to Everett. "Did you know about this too?"

Everett looked down at the ground.

"You should have been looking out for your sister."

"I know. I'm sorry. It was a stupid thing to do," admitted Everett.

Pepper piped up again. "I was the one who got us into

this mess. Everett tried to talk me out of it, but I wouldn't listen. He *was* looking out for me."

"And I guess that explains why we were going through so much food. That jar of pickles I was looking for the other day, is that where it went?" Grandma said.

Pepper nodded.

Grandma rubbed her forehead as if she had a headache, then said, "I'd better hear the whole story right from the beginning."

So Pepper explained how it had happened. She didn't tell the whole story, though. She left out the part about her strange dreams, and about how she had been planning to go to California with Ray and had given him all her bus money. And she left out how she had gone out in the storm the night he'd stolen Grandma's car, and how she had almost drowned. In fact, she left out quite a bit.

When she was done, she asked Grandma, "Will we have to go to jail for being accomplices?"

"Not accomplices," Everett interjected. "The correct term would be *accessories after the fact*."

Pepper took a deep breath in and out. "Whatever you call it. Could we go to jail?"

Grandma paused a moment before she replied. "No, I don't think so. You didn't know he was an escaped criminal, did you? So you don't have to worry about that."

Pepper considered this. Even if she hadn't known Ray was the escaped prisoner from Brannen Lake, she'd still helped him after she realized he'd broken a few laws: entering the country illegally, breaking and entering. Not to mention stealing a car. She wasn't guiltless. She knew that much.

"We'll have to report this to the police, though," Grandma went on to say.

Pepper felt the blood drain out of her face. She looked at Everett. He was pale as well.

Grandma was still talking. "This is a very serious matter. Everett, I want you to chop enough wood for the rest of the summer as punishment. And Pepper, from now on you will have to do all the washing up every night." She paused. "And we're going to have to tell your parents, of course."

It was the part about telling their parents that worried Pepper the most.

As they walked back to the shack, they passed Barry sitting on a log. He looked as satisfied as a fat bullfrog that had just swallowed a fly.

Supper that night was a tense and uncomfortable meal. Grandma said only a few words. It was obvious to Pepper, by the tightness in Grandma's jaw, that she was still upset. After supper Pepper washed the dishes without complaint. The thought of the stolen bus money weighed heavily on her. She'd promised Everett she'd look after it, and now it was gone. When it came time to buy the bus ticket to go home, she wouldn't be able to keep it a secret any longer.

After Pepper had dried and put away the last dish, she sat outside on the stairs and watched the sunset. The summer was going to be over before she knew it. Things had not turned out the way she'd hoped, she thought sadly. She'd let everyone down, and she was no closer to finding her real family.

CHAPTER 20

No Such Thing as Perfect

The following day Grandma made a suggestion. "Since I haven't got my car back from the police yet, and we can't drive into town, I think we all better walk over to the Fergusons. We can borrow their phone to call your parents."

Pepper's heart sank.

A short while later, Mr. Ferguson greeted them at his door. "Good morning. This is a nice surprise. How are things with you?"

"Not too bad, all things considered," said Grandma. "Did you hear the police found my car at the ferry terminal?"

"Well, that's good news! I'm glad to hear it. Would you like to come in?"

"Thank you. I have a favour to ask. I was wondering if we could use your phone? It's a few days past the due date for the new baby, and we're anxious to hear how things are going. Besides ..." She directed a significant glance

213

in Pepper and Everett's direction. "There are a few other things we have to fill them in on."

"Of course, of course." Mr. Ferguson beckoned them in. "I'll be out at the pool when you're finished. I brought some extra work home and was just going to take it out there and enjoy the sunshine."

While Grandma was dialing the number, Pepper felt a wave of anxiety. What would her parents say when they found out about Ray? She didn't want to be anywhere near the phone until she had to be, so she slipped across the living room and around the corner. As she tiptoed down the carpeted hall, she heard heated voices coming from April's room. They got louder as she drew nearer.

"You are going to stay in your room until you finish your homework. And that's that."

"But Mom, all my friends have the summer off."

"You should have thought about that last year at school. If you'd paid attention and worked harder, then you wouldn't have needed to go to summer school."

"I tried."

"You barely opened your books. You don't know what hard work is. You expect everything to be handed to you on a silver platter."

"That's not true."

"You certainly act that way. Sometimes you act like you're spoiled rotten. Ungrateful, too, for everything your father and I have done for you."

"What have you done for me? You and Dad don't even notice what's happening in my life half the time."

"That's nonsense. What about all the trips we've taken you on? The clothes we buy you? Anything you want, you get."

"That's just stuff. You want me to be a perfect little doll that you can brag about to your friends. It doesn't matter what I want. And when I'm having a problem, you don't want to hear about it."

"That's ridiculous."

"Oh, yeah? When's the last time we talked about anything that was important to me? And Dad? Dad is always busy with work. He never has time for me."

"If he didn't work hard, we wouldn't have this lovely home, the pool, the nice cars."

"I'd rather have a dad who wanted to be with me at least some of the time."

"April! That's enough out of you."

"You know what? I'm sick of everything. I'm sick of you and Dad. And I'm sick of all this homework!"

Suddenly a notebook flew out the door and hit the carpet with a thunk. The pages sprawled open. Pepper could see they were covered in doodles.

"Fine! Have your temper tantrum. But you're still not leaving your room until you finish your homework."

Pepper darted into the bathroom just in time. She heard April's mom come out of the room, pick up the notebook, toss it back inside, and slam April's door.

Pepper looked at her reflection in the mirror. So, the Fergusons were not a perfect family after all. Despite their life of luxury they still got frustrated, failed at things, and fought with each other. They were just like everyone else. Pepper closed her eyes. It felt like the room was shifting sideways. She braced herself on the countertop and looked in the mirror again. She ran some water on her hands, tried to smooth down her crazy curly hair, and then opened the door.

She found Grandma and Everett sitting on the pool deck with Mr. Ferguson. Mrs. Ferguson was bringing out a tray with tall cool drinks on it. She was smiling now, as if nothing had happened.

"Oh, there you are," Grandma said. "I called your parents, but no one was home."

Pepper concealed a sigh of relief.

"Would you like some pop?" said Mrs. Ferguson brightly, a perfect hostess smile on her face.

"Thank you." Pepper drained the glass, sucking thirstily on the straw. Then she popped one of the ice cubes in her mouth and sucked on it.

"Why don't you young folks have a swim?" suggested Mr. Ferguson.

"Sure. Thanks," said Pepper, standing up immediately. She was glad that today she was wearing her bathing suit under her clothes. "Come on, Everett. I'll race you to the end of the pool."

Everett glanced towards the house, then pulled off his T-shirt. Somehow he'd managed to stay as pale as he'd been at the beginning of the summer. But his arms looked a tiny bit more muscled, Pepper thought. It must be all the rowing he'd been doing.

Everett won the race, but only by an arm's length.

As they rested at the end of the pool, Pepper saw April come out.

"All finished, dear?" asked Mrs. Ferguson. There was a forced cheeriness in her voice.

"Most of it. I'll do the rest later."

April sat down at the edge of the pool. She dipped her feet in the water and slowly swished them back and forth. Then she pulled her feet up out of the water, crossed her arms on her knees, and laid her cheek down. The sun lit her hair and the side of her face, illuminating it like a painting.

"Let's go talk to her," said Pepper to Everett. "Race you back again."

Pepper pushed herself harder. This time she was going to win. When she reached the finish, she shoved the hair out of her eyes and looked around, gasping. Where was Everett? Then she saw him, still at the far end of the pool.

"Not much of a race," commented April.

"No," admitted Pepper. "He's a pretty fast swimmer when he wants to be, though." She tried to wave Everett over, but he pretended not to see her. He was struggling to pull himself out of the pool, the picture of awkwardness. "He's a little shy," Pepper added quickly. "But he's a nice guy when you get to know him."

"Yeah. He came over one day and gave me a little bird he'd carved. He didn't say much, hardly anything really, but it was still a nice thing to do."

Pepper squinted up against the sun trying to read April's expression. There was a sad, faraway look in her eyes. She could tell April wasn't thinking about Everett at all. Not only that, it looked like she'd been crying and was about to cry again.

"Is something wrong?" Pepper asked.

"No." April paused a moment. "I mean, yes. Everything's wrong."

"Like what?" Pepper had a pretty good idea April was going to start talking about the fight she'd just had with her mom.

April made a face. "You don't want to know."

"Sure, I do. You can tell me. I won't tell anyone else."

"Promise?"

217

"Promise."

April leaned closer. "The boy I like just went away. I'm probably never going to see him again."

April was talking about Ray! A strange high-pitched squeak came out of Pepper's throat, and she had to bite her lip to stop it. She hadn't given a thought to how upset April would be about Ray. But once the words had been spoken, it seemed obvious. April was heartbroken.

Pepper struggled with her own feelings, trying to figure out how to respond. When it came to romantic advice, she was certainly no expert. "You'll meet someone else," she finally said. "There are probably a lot of boys who want to go out with you."

"Not like him." April shook her head firmly. "He isn't like anyone else I know. He even wrote a song for me. No other boy has ever done that."

"A whole song?" Pepper exclaimed before she could stop herself.

"Oh, yes. It was a really nice one, too."

Pepper kept a straight face, but she felt a little twinge. Ray had never finished his song about her, at least as far as she knew.

April went on. "But it's not just this guy I'm upset about. There's a bunch of other stuff too. My dad is too busy working all the time to even notice me. My mom is always telling me what to do. And they both say I should smarten up."

"What do you mean?"

"I have to go to summer school because I failed some of my classes. Everyone says I'm not trying, but it's not that. I just don't get it. I'm not smart like other people. My spelling is terrible. I'm always getting things backwards. Homework takes me twice as long as it does for anyone else. Sometimes I feel like giving up." Tears were rolling down her cheeks now.

Pepper started to protest. "But you passed some courses, didn't you? So ..."

"It's the courses I failed everyone seems to care about. I try and I try, but what's the point? Mom and Dad say that I'm lazy. Lazy and spoilt." She glanced over at the adults talking in the shade. "They tell me they're fed up. They want me to stop complaining and just do it. Well, I can't just do it! That's the problem. Now I have to write an essay about the moon landing, and I don't know the first thing about it. I can't look it up in the encyclopedia, because it just happened. What am I supposed to do?"

Suddenly Pepper had an idea. "Maybe Everett could help you."

April shook her head. "I don't think anyone can help me."

"Everett could. He knows all about the moon landing. In fact, he knows a lot about everything ... and he likes you."

They both looked over at Everett. He was pulling his T-shirt back on, his elbows forming pokey angles.

"I don't know. It's a lot to ask ..."

"He wouldn't mind. Trust me. He'd love to do it." She put her hands around her mouth like a megaphone. "Everett!"

Everett hesitated. His face was sticking out through the neck hole like a turtle's. "What?"

"Come over here. April wants to ask you something."

Everett stuck the rest of his head through, pulled his shirt down, and walked over. He looked worried, as if he expected they were about to play a prank on him.

April hesitated. "I need to ask your help with something. You can say no if you want."

Everett sat down. He swallowed hard and his Adam's apple travelled up and down his throat.

Pepper would have liked to stay close by, but she knew an audience would only make him more nervous. She swam to the middle of the pool, rolled onto her back, closed her eyes, and let herself drift in the water. Every once in a while she opened one eye and looked over. April was doing most of the talking, and Everett was listening. Eventually Everett began talking too. Then April got up and went into the house. A minute later she came back with a notebook. The two sat together. Everett was talking more easily now. April was taking notes, nodding her head, and actually looking interested in what Everett was saying. April said something and laughed. And then Everett was laughing too.

Pepper couldn't think of the last time she'd heard Everett laugh. She closed her eyes again and smiled.

A little later Grandma announced that they'd better be on their way.

"Will you come back tomorrow after my class?" Pepper heard April ask Everett.

"Sure."

"But what about the tide? It'll be back up at that time of day."

"I'll borrow my grandma's rowboat," said Everett. "I can come over and help you every day if you'd like."

"Thanks. You're a nice guy, Everett, just like Pepper said you were."

Pepper snuck a look at Everett. He was blushing a little, but he looked pleased.

CHAPTER 21

A Small, Dark Moth

The next day Pepper felt bored and listless. A fog bank had rolled in, and the whole world felt muffled in a grey, dreary dampness. Everett had gone to the Fergusons' to tutor April. Grandma was off painting again. Chloe was grounded. There was no one left to talk to.

Then Pepper had one of her ideas. She climbed up over the bluff. Fog pressed in all around like a wet wool sweater. The cobwebs strung in the trees were heavy with dew. The only sound was the occasional mournful call of a faraway foghorn. Pepper peered through the mist over the other side, but it was too foggy even to see the roof of Chloe's shack. Pepper crept down the path and tapped on the back window, where she knew Chloe had her bedroom. A moment later the window opened and Chloe's face appeared. "Pepper!"

"Is your mom around?"

"No. She's down at the water rinsing out some buckets. But she'll be back any minute."

"How much longer are you grounded for?"

"A few more days. It's like torture being stuck in here! What kind of punishment did you get?"

"I have to wash and dry the dishes every night."

"What! That doesn't seem fair. You're the one who got us into all this trouble, and all you have to do is wash dishes? Look what happened to me!"

"I'm sorry, Chloe. I really am."

"I'm bored out of my mind in here. All I've been doing is reading old magazines. Hey, do you notice anything different about me?"

Pepper thought Chloe looked about the same as always, but she took a guess anyway. "Did you do something different with your hair?"

"Yes! I teased it to give it more volume. I read about it in one of my magazines. What do you think?"

"It looks a lot … puffier."

"Thanks," said Chloe as she primped her hair a little more. "What have I missed since I've been cooped up in here? Tell me everything."

"Everett's gone over to help April with her summer school homework. He's going to help her every day."

"You're kidding me. Do you think she likes him?"

"Maybe."

"Boy, I'm out of the picture for a couple of days, and the whole world turns upside down. Hey, wait a minute. Something *did* happen. Wait till I tell you. Guess who came by my window yesterday."

"Who?"

"Barry, that's who. Believe it or not, he came to apologize to me."

"Barry? Apologize?"

"I know! He said he was sorry that I ended up getting grounded. He actually seemed like he meant it too."

Pepper rolled her eyes. "Come on. You don't really believe that, do you?"

"I have to admit I feel bad for him, what with his dad being out of a job and all. He doesn't have any real friends. I'm not exactly sure why he went and told on us, but maybe he thought we'd gotten in over our heads with Ray. Maybe he had our best interests in mind."

Pepper looked at her friend dubiously. There was a long silence.

"Or maybe not," added Chloe. Then, suddenly, she stiffened. "Shhh! I hear my mom coming in. If she finds me talking to you, she's going to be hopping mad." And with that the window snapped shut.

When Pepper returned to the Periwinkle, she could hear Grandma talking to someone. The fog had thickened so much, she had to come right up to the porch to see who it was. A man in a blue uniform. A policeman! The same one who had taken the report about the stolen car.

"It's been quite an ordeal," Grandma was saying.

"Yes, ma'am. I'm sure it has." He passed the car keys over to Grandma. "We've left your car for you in the car park. It's all locked up. It's probably not a good idea to leave the keys in the car."

"Yes, thank you, officer. I certainly won't," said Grandma.

Pepper was about to turn around and look for a place to hide when Grandma caught sight of her. "Pepper! There you are! Can you come here, please? There's something you have to tell the policeman, isn't there?"

Pepper's heart did a somersault. They were both looking at her.

223

"Well … yes. I suppose there is," Pepper said reluctantly. Then she told her story. The condensed story, that is. She tried to tell it the same way she had the last time she'd told it. The policeman pulled out his notepad and took notes. When Pepper finished, he asked her a few questions. Pepper did her best to answer them honestly, without giving away more than she had to.

"Why didn't you come forward with this information before?" the policeman asked.

"I'm sorry, sir. I wasn't sure what to do."

He looked at her sternly. Pepper expected him to say she'd have to go to the police station with him. But he didn't. Instead, he flipped his notebook closed, put it back in his pocket, and said, "I'll add this information to the file when I get back to the office."

"Are you still going to be looking for him?"

"We'll keep our eyes open, but even with what you've told me, there isn't a lot to go on." He paused. "You know, Pepper, you put yourself in a situation that could have been very dangerous. You made several serious mistakes in judgment along the way. And all of this has been terribly upsetting for your grandma."

Pepper nodded, looking down at her feet.

"Promise me you won't do something like that again."

"I promise."

He took her hand and gave it a firm shake. "I'm glad to hear it."

About noon the next day there was a knock at the door of the Periwinkle.

"I wonder who that is," said Grandma to Pepper and Everett. They were seated at the kitchen table, and

Grandma was giving them a lesson in watercolour painting. Pepper felt a sudden twinge of trepidation. It might be the policeman coming back to get her. But when Grandma opened the door, Mr. Ferguson was standing there. He was beaming.

"The baby was born this morning," he announced. "I just got the phone call."

Grandma clapped her hands. "Oh, wonderful news! Come in. Come in. Sit down and tell us everything."

Mr. Ferguson had to stoop so he wouldn't hit his head on the door frame as he entered the tiny shack. He sat on one of the spindly kitchen chairs and stretched out his long legs.

"Is it a boy or a girl?" asked Grandma.

"A boy. A healthy baby boy."

"A boy! Isn't that something? We all thought it was going to be a baby girl."

"Have they named him?" Everett asked.

"Not yet. He's quite a big baby, just over eight pounds, with lots of brown hair. Your father called me as soon as he got home from the hospital."

"I can't wait to talk to them," said Grandma.

"The doctor said the mother and baby are both doing so well, they can go home by the end of the week."

"That's wonderful. We'll plan our next visit into town then so we can call them."

Despite herself, Pepper was excited by the news and curious to hear more. With some satisfaction, she realized she was still the only girl in the family.

After Mr. Ferguson left, Pepper made herself a cheese and tomato sandwich and wrapped it in wax paper. She asked Grandma if she could borrow one of the old quilts she'd seen tucked away on a shelf behind a stack of paintings. As she pulled the quilt down, a small, dark moth fluttered out of its folds. Pepper was startled at first but leaned in to examine it more closely. The insect had come to rest on a square of white canvas. Its wings, as delicately patterned as wood grain, had two black spots like eyes that seemed to be looking back at her. When she reached out to touch it, it flew away.

Pepper walked over to Ghost Island in the bright sunshine. She spread the quilt out on the gravel and sat down. It was a patchwork quilt, faded and frayed, smelling faintly of must. A tuft of white batting poked out through a broken seam. Pepper felt a little sad, a little wistful. It wouldn't be long before the summer was over, and she hadn't found her real family. Maybe she never would. A new baby had come into their lives, and that was going to take some getting used to. Pepper ate her sandwich and then sat running her hand absent-mindedly over the quilt's smooth satin and once-luxurious velvet. She tried to remember the words to the song that Ray had written for her, but only a few came to mind. She could hum a little snatch of the melody, but that was all. How easily Ray had slipped out of her life, just like the song. She gazed out towards the sea. The sun shone brightly on the water. The waves lapped in against the shore, a regular sound like breathing. Almost hypnotic.

Something stirred in a corner of Pepper's mind. All in a rush, she remembered. Way back at the beginning of the summer she'd had that strange fleeting image of a girl sitting on a patchwork quilt—just as she was now. Although it was the hottest part of the day, Pepper closed her eyes and felt a prickly sensation pass through her like a shiver.

Someone called her name. She turned to look, but no one was there.

A few days later Pepper met up with Chloe, who had finally been allowed out of the house again. They climbed up to their fort and were dismayed to find half of it had collapsed. Branches were strewn all over the rocks, and some of the logs had toppled down.

"What the heck?" Chloe exclaimed. "What happened to our fort?"

Pepper surveyed the damage with disbelief. "It looks like someone wrecked it. Maybe it was Barry."

Chloe shook her head. "I know Barry's a weird kid, but I don't think he'd do something like this. I bet it blew down in the storm that night you almost drowned. I haven't been up here since then. Have you?"

Pepper tried to think. "I came over the bluff to see you when you were still grounded. But it was so foggy then, I didn't see it."

"Oh, man! It's going to take a lot of work to fix this fort up again."

Pepper and Chloe got busy immediately. It took most of the day, but when they were finished they both agreed it had turned out even better than the first time.

At the end of the week, Grandma drove Pepper and Everett into town. On the back porch she spent several minutes searching through her purse for the door key. Pepper could barely stand still. A part of her was excited to get inside, rush to the phone, and hear more about the baby, but another part of her felt weighed down with worry. She couldn't stop thinking back to the day when they had tried calling her parents from the Fergusons' house. After that visit Grandma had taken Pepper and Everett to the store; purchased pens, paper, an envelope, and a stamp; sat them down on the bench outside the store; and made each of them write a letter explaining what had happened with Ray. They'd dropped the letters in the mailbox before they returned to Shack Island. Pepper hated to think what her parents' reaction would be. No matter how she had struggled with the wording of the letter—Ray running away from Brannen Lake and hiding out on Shack Island, how he'd tricked her so she would help him—it still sounded completely outrageous. Not to mention risky, and maybe even dangerous.

"Do you think Mom and Dad might have got our letters by now?" she asked.

"I'm not sure. They might very well have," said Grandma.

A mix of dread and anticipation swirled in the pit of Pepper's stomach.

Finally the key was found and the door was unlocked. Grandma immediately went to the phone to place the call. She gestured for Pepper and Everett to lean in closer when the call was answered.

"Richard? How are you? ... And Colleen? And the baby? ... Oh, good ... good ... that's wonderful ... Congratulations ... And the name? ... Rex? ... Sorry. I didn't quite hear ... Oh, Max! That's a nice name. I like that ... Colleen! How are you feeling?" Grandma talked on and on. Then she said, "Oh, you did, did you? ... Yes ... Yes ... Very strange. I didn't realize anything was going on. It came as a complete surprise to me ... No, they're fine."

Pepper chewed her lip nervously. They must have received the letters after all.

Finally Grandma said, "Oh, yes, they're right here." She passed the phone to Everett.

Everett asked who the baby looked most like. He asked if they had taken any pictures of him. Then he listened for a while, and his face grew serious. "I know … You're right. Sorry, Mom … Me too … Okay, here she is."

Pepper took the phone.

"Pepper?" Mom's voice came across the line.

"Mom?" Pepper said. It seemed like years had passed since they had talked. "Are you happy now that the baby is born?"

"Oh, yes … but I miss you."

"You do?" Pepper felt a rush of joy. She had not expected that those would be the first words she'd hear. She'd thought it would be all about the baby. Or how shocked her parents were by her letter.

"Of course I do. I miss you terribly. I can't wait to see you again."

"But I thought …" A painful lump had formed in her throat, making it hard for her to speak.

"What? What did you think?"

Pepper caught Everett looking at her. She scowled at him and turned her back and spoke quietly into the phone. "I thought you just cared about the baby now. I thought you'd sent me to Shack Island for the summer to get me out of the way."

"Oh, Pepper! It wasn't like that at all. Honey, I just wanted you to have a nice summer, that's all."

"But … I'm not even part of the family. I'm an outsider. I don't belong. And now with the new baby and all …"

"Of course you're part of our family. We love you!"

The lump in Pepper's throat grew bigger. "Even after

everything that happened this summer, everything I wrote in the letter?" she blurted out.

There was a long pause, and then her mother said, "I have to admit we were very upset when we read the letter. It was a dangerous situation, Pepper. You must realize that. I told Everett he should have known better. You too. When you come home, we'll talk about it."

"Are you mad at me?"

"No. I wouldn't say mad. Disappointed, though. And worried when I think about what might have happened. But I want you to know that, no matter what, we're always going to love you."

Pepper felt her muscles relax and her heart soften. She wanted to believe it was true. Still, a few niggling doubts remained. "But what about how I had to give up my room and move up to the attic?"

"Oh, honey, I know you were very fond of your room, and I'm sorry about that. But we have to have the baby nearby so we'll hear him in the night." She paused again. "Dad and I have a surprise for you when you come home."

"What is it?"

"Well, I wasn't going to tell you. It's supposed to be a surprise."

"No. No. Tell me now!"

"Okay. Well, while you've been gone we've fixed up your new room. I hope you like it. We cleaned it up and moved out all the old boxes. Dad made a built-in bed and dresser and a closet. We put up some pretty wallpaper, and I made new curtains and a matching bedspread."

"You did all that? For me?" Pepper was pleased they had worked so hard to make her happy. Even so, she had a strong suspicion the room was more to her mom's tastes than her own. She'd probably have to put her own touches on it when she got home.

"Of course we did, honey," her mom said. "I really hope you're going to like it. Your dad wants to talk to you now."

A moment later her dad's voice came on the line. "Pepper? Are you there?"

"Yes. It's me, Dad."

"How's my girl?"

"I miss you."

"I miss you too, sweetie. I can't wait to see you."

"I'm sorry about everything that happened."

"Well, you've been through a lot this summer. We'll talk it over when you get home. But are you doing okay?"

"Yeah. I'm okay."

Grandma tapped Pepper on the shoulder and pointed to her watch.

"Grandma says I better hang up now. Long distance, you know."

"All right, then. Bye, Pepper. Love you. See you soon."

"Bye, Daddy."

Pepper's hand trembled as she hung up the phone. A homesick feeling welled up inside her. She sniffed loudly, then wiped her nose with the back of her hand, straightened her shoulders, and turned around. She blinked away a few tears, but she was smiling.

CHAPTER 22

Almost Real

Grandma asked Everett and Pepper to help pick beans from the garden, then fill the water bottles with a hose. It was a hot day and they were thirsty by the time they'd finished, so she made them a pitcher of lemonade. They sat down at the kitchen table while Grandma glanced through a pile of newspapers.

"Oh, my! Look at this!" She pointed to the headline on a small story at the bottom of the front page. "*Escaped Juvenile Delinquent Back in Jail.*"

Pepper felt a shock run through her body.

Grandma squinted, trying to read the small print. "Where are my reading glasses?"

As Grandma fished through her purse, Pepper grabbed the paper and scanned the story quickly. Her heart did a somersault. She read the story again more slowly. It described how the red-headed male, who could not be identified because he was a juvenile, had escaped from Brannen Lake

232

and had been thought to be hiding out in summer cabins in the local area. In fact, he had been several hundred miles north, working at a dairy farm. The owner of the farm was quoted as saying he'd had no idea the young man was an escaped juvenile delinquent, and that he had been a hard worker and had never complained about getting up early to milk the cows. The man went on to say there was a job waiting for the boy if he wanted to come back when he got out of jail.

Pepper handed the newspaper back to Grandma. "It wasn't Ray. The guy they caught was working on a farm up north the whole time. Hundreds of miles away," she said, and she could hear the shakiness in her voice. Maybe Ray had been telling the truth about being a military deserter. Could that mean he was her real brother too?

"Isn't that something. I guess we were wrong about Ray," Grandma said after she read the story. "But we have to remember, even if he wasn't the boy from Brannen Lake, he was still in a lot of trouble. That fact doesn't change."

Everett spoke up. "But Ray's not that much different from Huckle. And you think Huckle's okay."

Grandma looked at Everett over the top of her reading glasses. "Huckle didn't break any laws."

"But don't you always say to stand up for yourself, and stand up for what you believe in? That's all Ray was doing."

Grandma opened her mouth and then closed it again. She thought for a moment. Then she took off her glasses and smiled. "You know something, Everett? You've got a point."

Pepper went out to the back porch and sat down on the steps in the sunshine. Her head was spinning like a merry-go-round. As the minutes went by, her thoughts slowed

233

down again, and she was able to focus more clearly. When she thought back, she couldn't remember why everyone had thought Ray was the boy from Brannen Lake. Of course, she knew she was always too quick to jump to conclusions. But this time it wasn't just her. Other people did it too.

"Pepper?"

Pepper turned and saw Everett holding a letter.

"It's for you," he said.

Pepper took the envelope. Her name was written on it in black ink with a strong hand. There was a return address in Vancouver she didn't recognize, and a phone number written underneath.

Everett was still standing in the doorway, watching her curiously. Pepper shot him a pointed look.

"Okay. I'll leave you alone," he said, turning and going back inside.

She stuck her thumb in the flap and ripped it open. The letter was several pages long. When she unfolded it, a bunch of bills slipped onto her lap. Money! Who was sending her money? She looked at the bottom of the letter for the signature.

"*Please forgive me. Ray,*" it read.

Pepper felt the air rush out of her lungs. She went back to the beginning of the letter and began to read.

Dear Pepper,

I am writing because I feel ashamed of myself and what I did to you. You must hate me right now. I guess I went about things the wrong way. But I can't change that now. All I can do is say I'm sorry.

The night I left the island there was that big storm, but I'd decided I was going, no matter what. I figured the storm might even work in my favour. No one else would be out on a night like that. And if anyone was watching for me they'd expect me to leave at low tide. So I found a boat and made it across. It was pretty rough going. The rest of it—borrowing your grandma's car, catching the ferry in the morning—went smoothly, just like we'd planned.

I made it to Vancouver and found the Committee to Aid American War Objectors, and the two Peters. The office was right where you said it would be. Actually, even though they call it an office, it looks more like a bombed-out warehouse. It's a big empty space with a couple of desks and a few old couches. A lot of people go there for help, draft dodgers and military deserters like me. It's sort of like a club. Everyone looks out for each other. One of the Peters is going to get me in touch with a lawyer who does work for free. He said things might not be as bad as I'd thought. We'll see about that. I sure hope he's right. Not only that, he put in a word for me, so I got a job down at the docks. I met a couple of other guys there, Jim and Graham, both draft dodgers, who are renting an old house a few blocks from the water. It's got an extra room upstairs they're letting me stay in if I chip in on the rent. Jim plays the drums and he has a couple of friends who are musicians too. They've been coming over after work for jam sessions. We might even get a gig downtown at a coffee house.

I'm thinking of this as a second chance, a fresh start. I want to make a better life for myself. So when I got paid, the first thing I knew I had to do was send you your money back. It's all there. You can count it.

There's something else that's been weighing on my mind. I know Everett had a crush on April and I should have stayed clear, but after I saw her that day through the binoculars I couldn't stop thinking about her. One day I decided to take a big

235

chance. I went along the beach and found her house. I waited until I saw her parents drive away and then I went and introduced myself. I liked her, and she liked me too. I went over there a few times after that, even though I was worried someone might see me. I was lucky. No one ever did. The night I left, I went to see April to say goodbye. She didn't want me to go, but I had to. It wouldn't have worked out anyway. She deserves someone who's got his life together. I hope she sees that.

When I left, I knew I had to do it on my own. I have to get myself on the right track again before I can be any good to anyone else. I'm sorry for not telling you I was going. But I never thought you coming with me was a good idea. Not just because it was risky and the police would be on our tail. I didn't want you to run away from your family. I don't think you realize how worried and scared they would have been. But you were so insistent, and I knew I wouldn't be able to talk you out of it. So that's why I left without telling you.

I know you also thought we could go to California to find our mom. Well, I have to confess something, and if you think I'm a jerk I don't blame you. You see, even if the lawyer can get everything cleared up, there's no point in going to California. Mom didn't move there. I'm ashamed to say it—but I made that up.

This is the hardest part of what I have to tell you. You see, I don't know what happened to your mother or your father. I don't know if you have any brothers or sisters. I'm not who you think I am.

When we met, I could tell how much you wanted me to be your brother. I went along with it at first because I figured you were more likely to help me that way. Not tell anyone I was hiding there. Bring me food. That kind of thing.

As I got to know you, though, I grew to care about you like

any brother would for his kid sister. When you asked about your family, I told you stories I thought you'd like to hear. The last thing I wanted to do was hurt you.

It probably doesn't matter to you now, but what I told you about me growing up in foster homes was true. My dad left when I was a baby. My mom drank, and they said she wasn't a fit mother. That's why I went into foster care. I know what it's like to feel you don't really belong. Not to have any family of your own. But you have to realize that, even if you never find your real family, you have an adoptive family who loves you. You don't know how lucky you are.

Even though we aren't related by blood, I'll always think of you as my little sister. I hope you'll write back to me and let me know how you are doing. I put my phone number on the envelope with the address too. But I'll understand if you don't want anything to do with me after all this.

I hope you get this letter. I had to look up your grandma's address in the phone book at the library. Well, that's about all there is to say. Besides, my hand is cramping up.

Please forgive me.

Ray

Pepper slowly folded up the letter. Her fingers were trembling. Then, on the back of the last page, she noticed something else.

P.S. I fell asleep this afternoon and had the weirdest dream. A girl was sitting on a beach. She was running her hand back and forth along a blanket, a sort of patchwork blanket, I guess you'd call it, and looking out towards the sea. The sun was glinting off the water. She turned and looked at me. And it was you.

*I don't know why I'm telling you this, but it woke me up,
and it left me with the strangest feeling. Almost like it was real.*
  R.

Pepper slid the letter back in the envelope. She stared straight ahead towards the houses across the street but was too deep in thought to notice any of them. She thought about everything in the letter, and the thing she kept coming back to was Ray's dream about the girl on the beach. She had never told him about the image that appeared to her on her first visit to Ghost Island. But it had turned out to be some kind of a premonition. *She* was the girl who was sitting on that patchwork quilt on the beach. And Ray had dreamed that very thing. Maybe even at that exact moment she'd been there. Up until now, it was Pepper who'd had strange ESP dreams about Ray. Now he was having dreams about her. She wasn't sure how ESP worked, but she did know one thing. It was an invisible thread that linked the two of them, sewing their lives together.

Pepper hugged the letter to her chest. Sure, Ray had made some mistakes in his life, but he wasn't all bad, either. He wasn't her brother, but that didn't matter as much as she'd thought it would. They had a different kind of connection, a mysterious one. Not a boy-crazy connection. It was something altogether different.

CHAPTER 23

The Last Campfire

The afternoon before Pepper and Everett were set to leave for home, Pepper sat on her bed in the Periwinkle and thought back to the day she'd arrived on Shack Island at the beginning of the summer. In one way it felt like years had passed. In another way, it seemed as if it was no time at all.

She picked up the carved fish Ray had given her and breathed in its tangy cedar smell. She placed it carefully back on the apple crate table. Then she turned her attention to her pen, which was also sitting on the tabletop. She concentrated as hard as she could. Surely, now that she had made a true ESP connection with another person, she must be able to get that pen to move. Yet it remained fixed to its spot, as if it had been glued there. Pepper leaned over and flicked the pen with her finger. It shot across the room, hit the curtain to Everett's room, and fell to the floor with a loud smack. She watched it land with bitter satisfaction.

239

Whatever power she had—ESP, mental telepathy, or something even more mysterious—was elusive. It never seemed to work the way she wanted it to. It came when she least expected it. It didn't seem to be something you could practise and get good at, the way her ESP book with the swirly psychedelic cover suggested. It remained, always, just a little bit out of reach.

Everett pushed the curtain aside. "What was that noise?"

"Nothing." Pepper considered Everett for a moment. He wore a sad expression, and suddenly Pepper knew what was wrong. "Are you going to miss April when we go?" she asked.

"Yeah," Everett admitted, blushing slightly. "She asked if I was going to come back next summer."

"What did you say?"

"I said I hope so."

"I think she likes you."

"Really?"

"Definitely." Pepper tried to think of something else to cheer Everett up. "Hey, how about we have a campfire tonight? It'll be the last one before we go. We'll invite Chloe. And Huckle and Starshine too. We can roast marshmallows." She jumped to her feet, picked her pen off the floor, and put it back where it belonged. She was eager to shake off the creepy feeling she got whenever she thought about ESP-related things too much.

Grandma made them a special supper for their last night on Shack Island: salmon, tomatoes and beans from her garden, and blackberry pie for dessert. Pepper washed, dried, and put away all the supper dishes. Then Grandma helped them make a fire on the beach. Huckle and Starshine rowed over and joined them. Huckle was excited about the music festival they'd been to.

"We saw the Flying Burrito Brothers and Strawberry Alarm Clock and the Grass Roots. It was totally far out. Tents everywhere."

"The Flying Burrito Brothers?" asked Grandma. "What are they? Trapeze artists?"

"No. An American band. They play country-rock kind of music. There were a lot of other bands there too. Rock 'n' roll bands. Some folk music. And thousands of people."

Chloe arrived after dinner and sat down on a log next to Pepper. Pepper had already told her about Ray's letter, so the first thing Chloe did was shoot Pepper a knowing look. Then she stuck a marshmallow on a stick, held it over the flames, leaned over, and whispered, "You know, I still think Ray's cute. Even after everything that happened." Before Pepper could react, Chloe's marshmallow dropped into the fire. "Darn it!" She took another marshmallow from the bag and speared it, then gave Pepper a playful poke in the ribs. "Hey! You still owe me an ice cream."

"Hah!" Pepper let out a pig snort and giggled.

Chloe giggled too. "You better come back next summer, 'cause I'm not going to let you forget about that."

Pepper pulled the hood of her kangaroo jacket up over her head. The evenings were noticeably cooler now. There was a crispness in the air. Over the past few days the leaves on the maple trees at the car park had started to turn yellow.

Huckle pulled his harmonica from his pocket and played a song. The campfire embers glowed orange. Pepper watched the flames dancing. Sand fleas jumped up against her bare ankles, and the smoke stung her eyes whenever the breeze blew in her direction. She poked her stick into the heat and watched her marshmallow steam, soften, and begin to turn brown.

After a while Barry came walking along the beach towards their campfire. He hesitated when he got closer.

"Come on over," called Chloe. She scooted along the log to make a space for him.

Barry sat down and shifted himself nervously.

Everett and Pepper looked at each other. Then Everett handed Barry a stick, and Pepper passed him the bag of marshmallows.

"Thanks," said Barry, allowing himself a small smile. He popped one marshmallow directly into his mouth, then poked another one into the fire.

Pepper looked out into the shadows gathering all around. It was hard to believe that tomorrow she was going home, that her summer on Shack Island had drawn to a close. She'd started out feeling exiled on this remote, rocky island with its hodgepodge of tumbledown shacks. But she didn't feel like that anymore. She'd grown fond of the place. She liked the way the weather-worn shacks showed their age, clinging like barnacles through years of wind and storms and the lash of the sea. She liked Grandma's mismatched kitchen chairs, the smell of salt in the air, and her little bed, where the sound of the waves lulled her to sleep every night. She didn't even mind the outhouse anymore.

She wasn't looking forward to saying goodbye to Grandma tomorrow. But she was eager to see the new baby. And she missed her mom and dad. It was home. She belonged there. She knew that now.

Before the summer, she'd thought she had the most boring family in the world. But Grandma lived on Shack Island each summer and painted pictures. Everett was practically a genius. Not only that, he had risked his life to save her from drowning during a storm. She had a new baby brother, and her parents had decorated the attic bedroom just for her.

Her family might not be flashy. They might not be glamorous. They might not take exotic holidays or drive air-conditioned cars. But the feeling Pepper got when she thought about them, and knowing they felt the same way about her, well ... that feeling was better than any fancy car could ever be.

Only one other campfire burned farther down the beach. Already some people had boarded up their shacks and left for the summer. Many of the shacks were dark. Pepper could still make out the dim shapes of the bluff, Middle Island, and Ghost Island in the dusk. She thought of the way the islands joined together under the water. Even when you couldn't see the connection, it was there.

Ray was part of her life now. Though they lived far apart, they would always be connected. She hoped things would turn out well for him, that he'd be able to make a good life for himself.

She would write to him. She might even phone him tomorrow from the bus depot in Vancouver. No matter what, she would always hold him close in her heart.

Overhead the first stars began to appear in the darkening sky. Then, out of the corner of her eye, Pepper saw a streak of light. A brief blaze, and it was gone. A UFO? Or a shooting star? Pepper hoped it was a shooting star. She thought very hard, then made a secret wish.

"Hey, your marshmallow's burning!" Chloe nudged Pepper with her elbow.

Pepper pulled her stick from the fire. She blew on her

marshmallow, pulled the blackened part off, and popped the rest in her mouth. If summer had a taste, this was it. It made her think of dragonflies, thistles, and sun-dappled shadows. And it melted in her mouth like a warm, lazy dream.

ACKNOWLEDGEMENTS

I would like to thank my editors, Barbara Pulling, Dawn Loewen, and Audrey McClellan, for their wisdom and gentle guidance. Many thanks as well to Frances Hunter for her beautiful design, and to my publisher, Diane Morriss, for her unflagging support and patience along the way. Finally, I wish to thank my husband, Adrian, and daughter, Katie, for their ongoing belief in this project and in me.

Although this story is fiction, the book Pepper finds on the bus is real: *How to Make ESP Work for You*, by Harold Sherman (New York: Fawcett Crest Books, 1964). Whether ESP is real is up to you to decide!

ABOUT THE AUTHOR

Penny Chamberlain has many fond memories of summers when she was growing up. Each year Penny, her sister, and her two brothers would spend part of the summer at their grandma's seaside cabin not far from Shack Island. Those pleasant memories from the 1960s and early 1970s were the inspiration for this book.

Penny was born in Nanaimo, British Columbia, and now lives in Victoria where she works in a hospital, coordinating Rehabilitation Services. *Shack Island Summer* is Penny's third book.

Also by Penny Chamberlain

The Olden Days Locket

From the moment she first
steps off the school bus, twelve-
year-old Jess is intrigued by
Point Ellice House. She feels
she knows what is around every
corner and behind every door
of the beautifully preserved
Victorian home. Her interest
and repeated visits impress the
guide in charge, and before long
Jess has a volunteer summer job
at Point Ellice House.

 Jess begins having visions
of a girl named Rose, visions that take her back in time to
a terrible streetcar accident. Now it's up to Jess to solve a
mystery and to ease the troubled spirit who has haunted the
area for so long.

• *Saskatchewan Young Readers' Choice Award* (*Nominee*)
• *Red Cedar Award* (*Nominee*)
• *Chocolate Lily Award* (*Nominee*)

HISTORICAL JUVENILE FICTION • 186 pp
ISBN 1-55039-128-3
Also available as an ebook

Chasing the Moon

Twelve-year-old Kit must
spend the summer with
her estranged father, whose
mysterious nighttime activities
and free-spending habits arouse
her suspicions. Then a strange
carnival boy enters the picture.
He has an eerie way with a
tarot deck that shakes Kit to the
core. Still, something about him
engages Kit, and, together, they
embark on a headlong journey
that will carry them from the
dark waters north of Victoria to the "blind pigs" of Seattle.
On the way, Kit will discover depths of insight she did not
know she possessed, and will win for herself one of her
dearest wishes.

- *Our Choice Award*
- *Chocolate Lily Award (Winner)*
- *Red Cedar Book Award (Nominee)*

HISTORICAL JUVENILE FICTION • 186 pp
ISBN 1-55039-157-7
Also available as an ebook